"I'll help, Molly...but it will cost you."

Derek felt a grin pull at his cheeks. "Lasagna. You can pay me with the amazing lasagna you make."

Molly's face reddened. "You want me to cook for you?"

"Well, I can help." Derek's suggestion surprised him as much as it had probably shocked Molly. "Think of it more as a working dinner."

She remained silent. Derek clung to hope. She could go either way. "I'll even do the dishes," he added.

Sweet laughter filled the room. "Okay. When do you want to do this?"

"How about tonight?"

Molly's eyes popped. "Seriously?"

"Yeah, we need to get your business booming in order to keep your store open. I want you to welcome Grace into your home and give her the life she deserves."

The idea of spending more time with Molly caused Derek's insides to vibrate like a rattlesnake's tail. But was that a good idea? Probably not. But he didn't care what his mind was telling him. For the first time in years, Derek was listening to his heart…

Weekdays, **Jill Weatherholt** works for the City of Charlotte. On the weekend, she writes contemporary stories about love, faith and forgiveness. Raised in the suburbs of Washington, DC, she now resides in North Carolina. She holds a degree in psychology from George Mason University and a paralegal studies certification from Duke University. She shares her life with her real-life hero and number one supporter. Jill loves connecting with readers at jillweatherholt.com.

Books by Jill Weatherholt

Love Inspired

Second Chance Romance
A Father for Bella
A Mother for His Twins
A Home for Her Daughter
A Dream of Family

Visit the Author Profile page at Harlequin.com.

A Dream of Family

Jill Weatherholt

LOVE INSPIRED
INSPIRATIONAL ROMANCE

LOVE INSPIRED®
INSPIRATIONAL ROMANCE

ISBN-13: 978-1-335-56711-6

A Dream of Family

Copyright © 2021 by Jill Weatherholt

Recycling programs
for this product may
not exist in your area.

This edition published by arrangement with Harlequin Books S.A.

For questions and comments about the quality of this book, please contact us
at CustomerService@Harlequin.com.

Love Inspired
22 Adelaide St. West, 40th Floor
Toronto, Ontario M5H 4E3, Canada
www.Harlequin.com

Printed in U.S.A.

And I say unto you, Ask, and it shall be given you; seek, and ye shall find; knock, and it shall be opened unto you.
—*Luke* 11:9

To my father, whose dedicated and loving role
as caregiver to my mother personifies
a real-life love story.

Chapter One

Past Due. Molly Morgan's hand trembled. The invoice with its bold red block-style font taunted her. Delinquent. Until recently, she'd never been late for anything in her life. She placed the piece of paper facedown on the counter along with the other late notices and scanned the room. Bound to Please Reads was the bookstore she'd dreamed of owning as a little girl. Would she lose her dream?

Books had saved Molly's life. She'd sought refuge in the dark closets of countless foster homes, hiding from the adults who'd taken her in for the money. There had been a few nice families, but her time in those homes had been short-lived. She'd learned early not to get attached.

Molly straightened her shoulders. She refused to think about the large chain bookstore that had recently opened its doors in a neighboring town. Within a week, their presence had quashed Molly's once impressive sales along with her hopes of adopting a child.

Outside, a truck's engine rumbled. A piercing beeping sound filled the room. Molly breezed across the store. Her long fiery-red hair brushed her slender shoulders. With her nose pressed to the front door, she spotted a white-and-orange truck, absent a logo, parked along the curb. She glanced at her watch. Strange. It couldn't be a delivery. Wilson's Hardware didn't open until nine thirty. The space on the other side of her bookstore had been vacant since the owner of Huggamugg Café had passed away. Was this the new tenant?

The driver's side door of the truck opened, and a long, jeans-clad leg extended to the pavement. Molly's heartbeat doubled in speed at the sight of a tall, broad-shouldered man stepping from the vehicle. Wearing tinted sunglasses and with a head of dark, wavy hair, the stranger held her attention hostage. *Whoa.* He had to be new in town or visiting. She would have remembered seeing him.

In four strides, the handsome man rounded the truck and opened the passenger side door. Her emerald-green eyes popped open. Wait— he wasn't a stranger. What in the world? No way! It couldn't be. But it was. Her stomach roiled. Cramming his hands inside the pockets of his fitted boot-cut jeans was Derek McKinney. Memories seared her brain. He was the reason she'd been left at the altar two years ago.

Seconds later, a chocolate German shepherd puppy bounded from the vehicle. The animal danced at Derek's feet while he removed a box from the seat and turned. Molly dropped to her hands and knees and then half laughed at herself. Why did she need to hide? He should be the one ducking. She pushed herself off the cold terrazzo tile, dusted off her hands and took another peek. Why was he standing in front of the vacant store next door with his face pressed to the glass? Unable to peel her eyes away, she watched as he placed the box on the ground and checked his watch. Next, he picked up the dog, gave it a quick peck on its forehead, and took it back to his vehicle. Although the kiss was sweet, Molly's stomach twisted when he headed toward her store.

Keep walking. The front door was unlocked for the day. Derek would see her if she attempted to relock the entrance. *Don't panic.* Running her hand over her head to smooth the flyaway hairs, she bit down on her lower lip, scurried toward the counter and squared her shoulders.

The bell chimed and footsteps tapped closer. Never in her wildest dreams had she imagined seeing Derek again. With her back to the door, Molly fingered through the nearby heap of papers from the adoption agency.

"Hello. I'm sorry to bother you, but—"

Derek's deep voice trailed into nothingness. Molly sucked in a breath and whirled around to face the man who'd ruined what should have been the happiest day of her life.

With saucerlike eyes, he strolled closer. His brow arched. "Molly? What are you doing here?" He half smiled and moved forward.

She could ask him the same question. Molly took a step back, but not before a whiff of his spicy aftershave tickled her nose. She refocused on the problem standing in front of her. This was her town. He didn't belong here. "I own this store."

"So you live in Whispering Slopes? That's great." Derek took in his surroundings, turned his icy-blue eyes back to her and flashed a smile.

Molly nodded and gripped the edge of the granite countertop. Why was he acting as though they were long-lost friends? Back in their college days, Derek had never showed interest in where she was from or anything about her. He'd been her fiancé's best friend, and she'd tolerated him. But she'd known the truth. He hadn't thought she was good enough for Ryan. Why the sudden interest? Did he feel guilty? Well, she hadn't just fallen off the turnip truck, or however the saying went. "Yes, since I was in junior high. So I should be the one asking you what you're doing here."

"I'm opening up a coffee shop next door." He pointed to the door. "It looks like we're going to be neighbors."

Was he joking? No. This couldn't be true. There had to be a mistake. Maybe she was dreaming. She pinched her arm. Nope. He was still here. Rats. "But my landlord said he was renting the space to a big-time franchise owner."

Derek's cheeks flushed. "I wouldn't call myself 'big-time,' but I do own quite a few shops."

Could her Monday get any worse?

The front doorbell tinkled for the second time.

Molly's stomach twisted when she spied her landlord, Rusty McAllister, stepping inside. Had he come with hopes of collecting his money? Over the past two months, her sales numbers had taken a dive, prompting his recent late notice. Guilt gnawed at her insides. Rusty had been a great friend to her adoptive mother. He'd also been a strong shoulder for Molly to lean on after her mother lost her battle to cancer three days after Molly was left at the altar.

"Just the people I was looking for. Hello, Molly." Rusty headed toward them and extended his hand. "You must be Derek. It's good to meet you in person, son." After they shook hands, he reached inside the pocket of his tan slacks. "Here's the key to your new space. I can speak for the entire community when I say we're thrilled you have decided to set up shop in Whispering Slopes. I've read a lot of articles on your expanding franchise. Your coffee is famous."

Unlike Rusty, Molly wasn't exactly doing cartwheels over her new neighbor. She bit her lip and hoped her landlord wouldn't inquire about her late rent payment in front of Derek.

"I'm happy to be here. If things go well, I'm hopeful I can sign a permanent lease agreement," Derek said before pocketing the key.

Molly's ears bent in the direction of Derek's response. Had he only signed a month-to-month lease? *Yes!* There was still hope. "So you're not sure you'll stay?" Her tone probably sounded giddy. But after what he'd done to her, why should she care what he thought?

"Mr. McAllister was kind enough to allow me some flexibility with the rental contract."

"Please, call me Rusty."

Derek nodded. "Rusty agreed to give me some time to test the market demand in the area."

Molly's hopes popped like a quick pinprick to a balloon. The locals in Whispering Slopes lived for their coffee. After Huggamugg closed, everyone in town flocked to Buser's General Store for their caffeine fix. Poor Elsie Buser, Molly's mother's best friend, struggled to keep up with the volume. Molly had no doubt Derek's store would be successful.

Rusty leaned against the counter. "That's something I need to talk about with both of you." Her landlord's brow furrowed.

Molly had known Rusty since she'd first moved to Whispering Slopes as a teenager. Something was on his mind.

"Let's take a seat." Rusty pointed to a nearby table with four cushioned straight-backed chairs.

Derek pulled out a seat and motioned to Molly.

She prepared for the worst. "Thank you," she muttered and sank into the chair. The two gentlemen followed her lead.

"What's up, Rusty?" Derek splayed his hands on the table.

Rusty turned his attention away from her and

onto Derek. *Phew*. He wasn't going to address her struggles with her rent. At least not today.

Rusty cleared his throat. "Derek, the day after you signed your lease, I received a phone call from a real estate developer interested in my property. He has this idea about turning it into office space. He's part of a large company investigating some commercial properties in and around the Shenandoah Valley. Several months ago, I put out a few feelers since I hope to retire in the near future. When I didn't get any interest, I thought your plan to not get locked into a long-term lease would be perfect for both of us. I know you want to buy some time to see if your coffee shop produces a generous profit, and if it does, you're interested in purchasing both of my stores. You also mentioned a specific dollar amount you would be willing to pay."

Molly gasped out loud. "Both?" Derek wanted to buy the real estate he planned to rent and the space that housed Bound to Please Reads?

Derek looked at Molly before nodding to Rusty. "That's my plan. I feel it's time to expand my investment portfolio."

"I want to be up-front with you, Derek. The developer's offer is substantially more than yours, but I have other things to take into consideration." Rusty paused and glanced at Molly before he continued. "Since the investor's offer will expire in thirty days, we all have some time to see what happens. Fair enough?"

Derek extended his hand. "Works for me. Thank you, sir."

So Derek could be her landlord? This day was getting worse by the minute. It was one thing to have Derek running his shop right next door to hers, but paying him rent? Of course, it was a moot point. At the moment, she didn't have the money to pay either man.

Molly's shoulders slumped. Seeing Derek again had triggered a flood of painful emotions from her past, feelings she'd struggled for so long to forget. She couldn't allow Derek to reopen those old wounds. And becoming her landlord—no way. But what other choice did she have? As much as she didn't want to admit it, having Derek as her landlord would be better than losing her store and having it turned into office space. Maybe she could try to get a loan and purchase her shop? If she didn't find a solution, everything she'd worked so hard for, everything she loved, would be lost. And what about her plans to adopt? Would the adoption agency give a child to someone with no income?

Derek stepped inside his latest investment, Insomnia Café. He closed the door and fell back against the glass. Releasing a slow and steady breath, he shoved his hands deep inside his pockets. *Molly Morgan.* Could the world get any smaller? He closed his eyes, and his mind flashed back two years to the stunning, hopeful bride.

It had been a perfect June afternoon, and the day had belonged to Molly. Her wedding day. There was no forgetting her gorgeous red hair swept off her shoulders with a demure clip. But a lace veil draped over her flawless porcelain skin couldn't hide the tears he'd seen running down her face after Ryan had whispered in her ear in front of the entire congregation.

Guilt gripped Derek's insides. He owned those tears, and he'd never forgotten them. On numerous occasions, he'd wanted to call Molly to explain. But back then, he'd turned away from God. It had been a dark time. If only he could turn back the clock.

Twenty minutes later, in the back of the store, Derek filled the water dish for Duke, his three-month-old shepherd. "Yeah, I know you're thirsty, bud." He placed the bowl on a rubber floor mat. A rap at the door sent Duke racing to the front of the shop. Derek followed and spotted Rusty peering through the window. Welcoming the company to help erase his thoughts of the past, he opened the door. "If you've come for a cup of coffee, you're early. My new equipment hasn't been delivered."

The older man shuffled inside like a swarm of bees were on his tail. "I've already had my two cups for the day." He glanced down at the dog jumping against his leg. "Well, who is this little fella? You sure are energetic."

"This is Duke." Derek smiled. "He's a rescue puppy."

"It's nice of you to take him in." Rusty scratched the animal behind its ear. Once the old man pulled his hand away, Duke ran to his bowl of water, his oversized paws sliding out from under him. The man directed his focus back on Derek. "Do you have a few minutes? There's something I need to speak with you about." He paused and took a breath. "It's more of a favor for Molly."

Rusty's solemn expression caused a knot of uneasiness to take hold. Was Molly in trouble? It wasn't his place to pry, so Derek remained silent.

"I won't take up too much of your time. I know you're busy, but I hope you can help me out, son." Rusty tipped his head toward a table in the corner of the room, next to a window.

"Sure, what's up?" Derek took a seat, and Rusty followed his lead. The morning sun streamed through the window, creating a glare off the tabletop.

"I've known Molly since she was a young girl. She's like a daughter to me. Her adoptive mother, Shelley, was a wonderful person and a dear friend of mine. Before she passed away, I made a promise I would keep an eye on Molly. Shelley didn't want Molly to ever struggle financially like she had." Rusty ran a hand across his forehead.

"Molly seems pretty independent to me."

The landlord laughed. "Bullheaded is more like it. But you're right. The problem is she's never been able to ask for help, even when she needs it. She wants to do everything on her own."

"I guess there's nothing wrong with being self-sufficient."

"True, but sometimes we all need help." Rusty paused and scanned the room before turning back to Derek. "You're obviously a brilliant businessman, Derek. I've read articles about the growth of your franchise in this part of the country. I think you could help her. Please know, I'm not one to gossip, so what I'm about to share with you is out of my concern and love for Molly."

Derek nodded in understanding.

"Through no fault of her own, her store is

in trouble. Big trouble," Rusty shared in a hushed tone.

Derek considered the man.

"She's up against the big guys. A large chain bookstore opened nearby a couple months ago. Molly won't discuss it with me, but I know her sales have declined because she's behind on her rent. I thought you could take a closer look at her operation. Give her some suggestions on how she could increase sales," Rusty pleaded.

Derek tightened and released his fists. He was the last person in the world she'd go to for help, but how could he say no to Rusty? The old man clearly cared so much for Molly. "I'm not so sure Molly would want my assistance." He blinked. "We have a history that I think she'd rather forget."

"Earlier, Molly told me you were Ryan's best friend, but it's all in the past. She needs help. I think she might be desperate enough to listen to your advice. If she doesn't turn things around, I'm afraid she might have to shut down her store."

His relationship with Ryan was definitely in the past. They hadn't spoken since the day of the wedding. Derek had heard through a mutual friend that Ryan was having doubts about getting married weeks before the wedding. Derek always wondered why he never shared his feelings with his best man. "Could that impact my offer?" Derek questioned.

Rusty's brow puckered. "If Molly doesn't start to turn over a profit in the next thirty days, I'll have to sell, whether you're ready to make a deal or not. I'm sorry, Derek, but I have to protect my future. And Molly will have to start over."

Derek couldn't fault the man. You couldn't be successful in business if you didn't make some tough decisions from time to time. "If you don't mind me asking, how much higher is my competition's offer?"

"I'll be honest with you. This developer has deep pockets, son. The amount you mentioned doesn't come close. If you can help her get back to making a steady profit, I would be willing to take an offer that is eighty percent of what the developer is willing to pay. If I know Molly can stay in business, I can retire with peace of mind and know I kept my word to her mother. If her shop is going to close anyway, I might as well take the larger offer right away instead of dragging it out and giving Molly false hope."

Rusty named the number, and Derek nodded. "I'll do what I can to help her." It was the least he could do, especially if Molly's failure could impact his plans for expansion within the Shenandoah Valley. Assisting her could buy him more time. He had a good feeling about this town and the positive effect it could have on his franchise. A hunch. And so far, those feelings had yet to fail him when it came to his business.

"I appreciate your help, Derek. But whatever you do, you can't let Molly know I came to you about this. I'm not one to keep secrets, but the last thing I want is for her to think I don't have confidence in her ability to run a successful business." Rusty extended his hand. "Her independence means a lot to her."

"Mum's the word." Derek shook hands with his landlord.

"I'll let you get back to work." Rusty pushed himself away from the table. "So I guess I'll see you at the chamber of commerce meeting on Thursday night. I heard the mayor already reached out to you."

"Yes. He did ask me to speak to the members. I'll admit, I was surprised to hear from him before I arrived in town."

Rusty laughed. "Word travels fast in a small town."

"I look forward to meeting everyone."

Rusty nodded. "Have a good day, son."

Alone in the store, Derek replayed the conversation in his mind. Not only did he have to work to get his business off the ground, but he needed to help Molly. He'd given Rusty his word. No way would he be like his father and break a promise. If he turned things around for Molly and could come up with the money he and Rusty had agreed to, maybe he and Molly could both have financial success in Whispering Slopes. Who knew, she might be able to forgive him for ruining her wedding day and her future.

Then again, suspicion had been written all over her face when he'd entered her store earlier. She suspected he'd played a role in breaking up the wedding. The last thing on Molly Morgan's mind was forgiveness. Getting her to accept his help would be about as easy as giving a cat a bath.

Chapter Two

"Molly! Hey, I tried to call you last night." High-heeled shoes pecked against the concrete outside the bookstore.

Molly turned to see Annie Preston. She moved at a brisk pace down the sidewalk, toting a leather briefcase and carrying a thick manila file. Her long, dark ponytail swung back and forth while her suede skirt swished against her knees. Annie was a social worker with the local adoption agency and had been assigned to work with Molly as she pursued adoption. Close in age, they'd become good friends.

Molly clutched her coffee cup. Exhausted after Derek's surprise appearance yesterday, followed by a long day of work and number crunching, she'd crawled into bed with her latest romance novel. If she couldn't have her own happily-ever-after, she could at least escape into someone else's perfect relationship. "I went to bed early."

Annie squinted into the sun and removed her sunglasses from the top of her head. "Did you get my message?" She slid the glasses over her eyes.

Molly reached inside the pocket of her white jeans and fished out the key to the front door. "No. Not yet." Molly didn't want to admit to her friend she'd been too overwhelmed by her financial situation to check her voice mail this morning.

Annie's face ignited in a smile. "I've got a file I'd like for you to take a look at."

"You do?" Excitement coursed through Molly's veins, and Derek's presence in town escaped her mind.

"Yes. The last home assessment went well. We're ready to proceed with the placement process."

"So that means you have a child in mind?" Her pulse increased. She'd been waiting for this moment.

"Yes, and I think she might be perfect for you. She's currently staying in our group home since things didn't work out with the previous foster parent." Annie passed the file.

"It's a girl?" Molly's heart soared. Was this

going to happen? Would she finally have a family of her own?

"Yes. And she's adorable. She's six years old, and her name is Grace."

Grace. A shiver traveled through her body. Molly knew God had handpicked this child for her.

"Why don't you take a look at the file, and maybe I can bring her by the house on Thursday night. Does that work for you?"

"I have the chamber of commerce meeting that evening. The mayor said he has some exciting news to share, so I shouldn't miss it." The thought of listening to Derek speak wasn't at the top of her list of things to do, but with her business struggling, missing out on major town news wasn't an option. "Can we do it tomorrow evening? The teacher has a conflict, so Book Buddies won't be meeting."

Annie pulled her cell from her briefcase and tapped the device. "That will work. Let's say around seven o'clock."

Molly loved Annie's demeanor. She took things in stride, never sweating the small stuff. Molly, on the other hand, sweated everything, especially now since Derek had moved in. "Sounds like a plan. Should I cook something for dinner?"

"I thought dessert might be better for the first meeting."

"Okay. That works for me. Do you know if Grace has any allergies?"

Annie laughed. "I knew you had a motherly instinct. Good for you for asking, but no, she doesn't."

"Great. I'll make my mother's delicious German chocolate cake. It has nuts in the icing. That's why I asked." Molly stepped forward and hugged Annie. "You're the best. Thank you so much for dropping this off. I'll see you tomorrow."

"You got it." Annie spun on her heel and hurried down the sidewalk.

Thoughts swirled through Molly's mind as she stepped inside the bookstore. A girl. She'd known the adoption process would require a great deal of patience to go through all of the proper procedures. When she'd started, she'd been in a good place financially. The bookstore had been open over a year and had a steady stream of customers. Profits had been up, and she'd been confident the store would continue to be successful. She'd also sold a few short stories to a magazine that had compensated quite well. The novel she'd been working on had been put on the back burner since her life had been turned upside down by her most fierce competition. She refused to quit without a fight, though. She'd get her numbers back in the black, so she didn't need to mention the decline in sales to Annie. She could do this.

Unable to wait, she glanced at her watch. There was plenty of time to take a quick peek at the file before opening the store. With the information held tight against her chest, she scurried back to her office and took a seat at her desk. Her fingertips traced circles on the folder. Could her future be inside? Molly was ready to meet Grace—at least on paper.

Her hands trembled as she opened the file and read the cover page. *Grace Williams.* Molly's eyes scanned the background information. Grace had been in foster care since she was an infant. *Just like me.* Molly's drug-addicted mother had left her in a back alley of the busy restaurant district in Chicago, along with a letter explaining why she couldn't keep the baby. Molly continued to read the details of how Grace had been abandoned on the steps of a church. Grace's birth mother, who later came forward and gave up all rights to Grace, was sixteen years old. *Just like my birth mother.*

As an infant, Molly had become a ward of the state. The similarities between her and

Grace were chilling. With the tip of her tongue, she moistened her finger, then flipped to the next page. Molly gasped for a breath and her heart slowed. Haunting deep blue eyes stirred memories. Molly knew that look. It was a reflection of her former self. Grace's expression told a story of pain and suffering experienced in her brief time on earth. The painted yellow walls of her office closed in. Molly slammed the file shut. *Lord, help me. Can I do this? Am I strong enough to help this child?* Suffocating thoughts swirled in her mind, stealing her air.

Seconds later, a calmness took hold. Shelley, Molly's adoptive mother, had come to Molly's rescue the summer before starting middle school. Shelley had saved her life and taught her the meaning of family. It was Molly's turn to do the same for Grace. She closed the file. A lightness filled her chest. This was God's plan. She turned her gaze toward the window, and until it was time to open the store, she pictured herself fluffing Grace's veil on her wedding day.

On Wednesday afternoon, the German chocolate cake was cooling on Molly's stove top. By the time Annie brought Grace by, it would be ready for the icing. With the tea kettle on the stove and filled with water, she turned on the burner. Molly stepped into the pantry to retrieve her leather-bound journal from her tote bag and took a seat at the kitchen table to make a few notes for her next Book Buddies meeting.

The project was near and dear to her heart. Soon after the grand opening of her bookstore, Molly partnered with several elementary schools in the Valley to form the book club. Every Wednesday after school, children gathered at her store to discuss books. Her goal was to promote the importance of developing a reading habit at an early age. Plus, the parents shopped and often made a purchase, which provided a bump in her sales. Molly was grateful for their support.

The tea kettle whistled, and Molly eased out her chair. She removed a large red mug from the cabinet, dropped a tea bag inside and poured the steaming water. She took a sip with hopes of settling her nerves before meeting Grace.

Her stomach fluttered at the sound of the doorbell's chime. She glanced at the clock on the microwave and flinched. After seven? Where had the time gone? Her pulse clamored in her chest as she moved toward the front door, tugging on the peasant blouse hanging loose over her skinny jeans.

"Sorry we're running late. We got caught

behind a tractor moving an oversized load," Annie announced when Molly opened the door.

Molly's breath caught in her throat when she saw the child. It was love at first sight. Her heart was no longer her own. Grace's striking blue eyes studied Molly. With a quick movement, the child turned her focus to the floor.

"Come in, please." Molly motioned for them to enter.

Annie made the introduction. "Grace, this is Molly Morgan."

Her knees felt like saltwater taffy forgotten in the August sun. She struggled to maintain her balance. Molly knelt in front of the child and extended her hand. "Hi, Grace. I've been looking forward to meeting you." *Don't get too attached.* But the words spinning in her head couldn't control her heart. Disbelief and hope collided when their fingers touched.

"Hi, Miss Molly." The little girl's voice was barely a whisper.

Don't cry. Do not cry. This is only a test. But she didn't want it to be a test. She wanted this child in her life. From the moment she saw the photograph of Grace, she knew God had answered her prayers. Molly wanted to take this child into her arms and protect her. She longed to welcome her with love to her forever home. But she knew she needed to give Grace time.

"Something smells delicious." Annie looked down at Grace and smiled. "Don't you think so, Grace?"

The child nodded. Her honey-colored hair skimmed her shoulders.

"It's our dessert. German chocolate cake. Do you want to help with the icing, Grace?" Molly dreamed of spending hours in the kitchen, sharing stories like a real mother and daughter.

"Okay," Grace chirped.

Molly led Annie and Grace toward the kitchen. She was relieved she'd held off on icing the cake. It would give her something to do with her hands. Plus, it might put Grace at ease rather than sitting around a table with two adults asking questions.

"Can I get you some tea, Annie? There's hot water on the stove. Grace, would you like some juice?"

"Tea sounds perfect." Annie placed her hand on Grace's shoulder, and the child huddled close by her side. "Juice for you?"

Once again, Grace answered with a nod.

What if Grace didn't like her? Was that why she wasn't talking? Molly retrieved a glass and coffee mug from the cabinet.

"I can make my tea, Molly. You and Grace go ahead and get started on the icing. I have a mound of paperwork to keep me busy." Annie poured water from the kettle into the mug before tossing in a tea bag. "Do you mind if I work at the table here?"

"No, go ahead. Make yourself at home." Molly's shoulders relaxed. Maybe she wouldn't be under the microscope. She pulled the juice out of the refrigerator and poured until the glass was three-fourths full. Molly passed it to Grace. The child pointed at the cartoon mouse heads covering the glass, and the sweetest giggle bubbled from her lips.

Molly's heart soared. "My mother bought me this when she took me on my first trip to Disney World. What can I say? I fell in love with Mickey." For a second, Molly thought she'd broken through the wall that Grace had built around her. Molly knew all about those walls. She'd constructed a few of her own as a child. But Grace's smile slipped away.

While Annie tapped away on her laptop, Molly removed the eggs and butter from the refrigerator. Next, she moved to the pantry to gather the vanilla, a can of evaporated milk and a bag of coconut flakes. Molly took note of Grace eyeing the bag.

"Do you like coconut?" Molly pointed to the flakes.

Grace's eyebrows twitched before she smiled. "Yes."

Molly opened a nearby drawer and pulled out a pair of kitchen scissors. With one snip, the aroma of coconut filled the air. "I have a yummy recipe for coconut chocolate chews. We can make them together sometime. Would you like that?"

Grace smiled and looked at her. "I love chocolate, too."

Molly wished she could bottle the feeling pulsating through her body as she imagined a future with Grace. "Let me get the step stool for you so you can stand at the counter and help me. Would you like to do that?"

Grace nodded and took a sip of her juice before placing the glass on the countertop.

Molly unfolded the stool and tapped her hand on the black nonskid plastic covering the top. "Hop on here, sweetie."

Grace flinched and focused her eyes on Molly.

Molly's jaw tightened. Was she moving too fast, calling her sweetie? Did that make Grace feel uncomfortable? But then a slight smile moved across Grace's lips. If Molly had blinked, she would have missed it. Yet she'd seen it with her own eyes, and for the second time tonight, Molly's heart ignited with joy. It was a first step, right? They needed each other. They were meant to be mother and daughter. She would do everything in her power to make sure that happened.

Thursday morning, after little sleep from the excitement of meeting Grace the previous evening, Molly sat hunkered inside her office at the back of her store. She recalculated her sales figures from last week for the fifth time. Squeezing her eyes shut, she hoped for a larger number when she refocused on the computer screen. *That can't be right.* But she knew the numbers didn't lie. Since the new chain bookstore had opened, her weekly sales had been on a downward trend. Her chest tightened. She'd have to go to the bank today to ask about taking out a small business loan. Rusty would be at the chamber of commerce meeting tonight. How could she face him without paying the rent she owed?

The alarm on her phone sounded a reminder. With only a half an hour before the store opened, she hadn't had a drop of caffeine to drink. Since Huggamugg had closed its doors, Molly made coffee at home, but this morning, she'd been in such a hurry to work on her invoices. Over the past few days, she'd seen the new equipment and supplies delivered to Derek's shop. Yesterday, when she'd spotted the Open for Business sign and a rush of customers, realization settled in. Along with a stomachache. Derek's presence hadn't been a bad dream. In desperate need of caffeine and against her better judgment, she pushed away from the maple desk and headed next door.

The cobblestone sidewalks outside of Insomnia Café bustled with activity. Molly leaned forward and peered through the window. She spotted Derek behind the counter, preparing orders for several customers. A handful of locals sat at the bistro tables. He'd only opened for business yesterday, and the place was packed this morning. Inhaling a deep breath, she pulled the door open, and the bell overhead chimed. Inside, she was greeted by the invigorating aroma of fresh brew.

"Good morning. Welcome to Insomnia." Derek called out without pulling his eyes away from the task at hand.

"Hello, Molly," a familiar voice called out.

At the end of the counter, her landlord waved. Molly raised a hand. "Hi, Rusty." She moved toward him. "I wasn't expecting to see you until tonight." With a crowd of people milling about, she wouldn't mention the check she owed him.

"I had to come and show support for my newest tenant." Rusty tilted his head in Derek's direction.

Molly still couldn't believe Derek was her new neighbor. For the past several nights, she'd tossed and turned, wondering how in the world this was possible. She could only hope once he opened Insomnia, he'd decide against purchasing Rusty's property. But then one of those big-city developers could swoop in and kick her out on the street. Her shoulders tightened. Why did Derek have to be the better option?

"What can I get you, Molly?" Derek called out.

"I'll have a large black coffee to go." The sooner she could make her escape, the better.

"Late night?" He glanced her way and winked.

"Not really." Truthfully, it had been the best night of her life. Wait. Was it her imagination, or did he look more handsome today? The sleeves of the blue Oxford shirt he wore were rolled up to reveal his arms. Had they always been so muscular? She shook off the thought and turned to Rusty. "So, what's on the agenda tonight?"

"We have a guest speaker." Rusty poured a splash of creamer into his brew.

"Anyone I know?" Molly placed her credit card on the counter.

"This is on the house." Derek slid the plastic back to her.

Molly shook her head and pushed the card closer. "Thanks, but I'll pay."

"Suit yourself." Derek reached over, grabbed the card and inserted it into the machine. He swiped the plastic and looked up. "To answer your question, the mayor invited me to speak tonight."

Oh great. She'd never been asked to speak at the meetings. Of course, she wasn't the king of coffee, either. Molly looked around. Customers jammed the place. When the payment machine made a strange noise, Molly glanced down at the screen. Declined.

Derek's soft glance reflected understanding. "Please, there's no charge. This machine has been temperamental this morning," he whispered.

Molly kept her focus on the counter. Her cheeks burned. How could she not afford a cup of coffee? She'd paid her credit card bill last month. But then she remembered she'd used the card to pay for her furnace service a couple of weeks ago. It wasn't cold enough to turn on the heat, but she wanted to be prepared. Molly appreciated how Derek handled the embarrassing predicament. She looked to him, smiled and took her beverage. "Thank you."

The front door was flung open, causing the overhead bell to ring. Molly spun around and spied Auntie Elsie buzzing across the floor, carrying a plate covered with tinfoil. A sweet aroma swirled in the air. Her auntie had been up early doing what she loved. Baking.

"Hello, sweetheart." She placed the treat on the counter and gave Molly a hug. "I wanted to come and say welcome." She focused her eyes on Derek. "We are so pleased to have you join our family, Derek."

Molly looked at the woman. Family? She glanced at Derek, who wore the charming smile he'd always flashed at the girls when they were in college. Family would never do what he'd done to her on the day of her wedding. Ryan and Derek never saw her outside of the church nursery, but she'd overheard their conversation. There was no denying what she'd heard. Derek had told Ryan he shouldn't marry her.

"Derek is our town's newest merchant. And a successful one, I might add. We are pleased to have him join our community." She turned to Molly. "You know, Whispering Slopes is a tight-knit town. We may not all be related by blood, but we look out for each other like our own. That's how it's always been."

Molly released her breath. She hoped Derek had no plans to become a permanent resident. He didn't belong here. This was her town.

Derek's lips parted into a slow and easy smile. "Aren't you the sweetest? Are you the Welcome Wagon?"

"I'm so sorry, young man. Where are my manners? I'm Elsie Buser. I own and operate Buser's General Store. If there's anything you need, drop by anytime. I'm a hop, skip and a jump up the street."

"Thank you. I appreciate it." Derek lifted a brow to Molly. "So you two are related?"

Mrs. Buser moved closer and locked arms with Molly. "Not by blood, but love. She's my best friend's only child." Her eyes twinkled as she leaned in to Derek. "And she's single, too."

"Aunt Elsie!" Mortified, Molly dipped her chin and stared at the floor. The last thing she wanted was for Derek McKinney to know anything about her personal life.

"I'll keep it in mind. It was nice to meet you, Elsie." He turned on his heel and headed to the end of the counter to tend to the next person in line.

Aunt Elsie placed both hands on her cheeks. "Oh, if I were thirty years younger."

Ignoring her aunt's swooning state, Molly reached for her cup of hot brew. She closed her eyes for a second. They shot open when she pictured Derek in a dark tuxedo, standing at the front of the church with her fiancé at his side.

"Rusty mentioned you and Derek already knew each other." A questioning look flashed across her aunt's face.

Molly knew her well. It was only a matter of time before she learned Derek was responsible for ruining her wedding. Aunt Elsie was like an archeologist. She could dig up information no one else would find. "He's Ryan's best friend." Were they still friends? Truth be told, she didn't care. It had been two years since she'd seen or heard from her ex-fiancé. She'd worked hard to leave the past behind her, but now it stared her in the face. She needed to make her escape. "I have to go open the store." She hugged Elsie without waiting to see her reaction and bolted toward the door.

"We'll see you tonight, Molly," Rusty announced as she hurried out of the shop before anyone could see her tears.

Outside, she sucked in a deep breath of the crisp air and wiped her eyes. She sighed. How could she be approved to adopt a child when she couldn't buy a lousy cup of coffee? Obtaining a loan might be her only hope if she couldn't turn things around soon.

Later in the evening, merchants from a wide array of businesses in Whispering Slopes filled the library. Derek kept his eyes peeled for Molly. Time was of the essence if he was going to help her business and expand his own. After a successful grand opening yesterday, he believed his coffee shop would continue to produce a generous profit. But what about Molly's store? If she didn't turn a profit soon, Rusty might go ahead and sell.

Scanning the room, Derek recognized a few people who'd come by his store to welcome him after he'd opened his doors. Most had been friendly and eager to ask questions about his accelerated rise to fame as a successful entrepreneur. At times, he couldn't believe it himself. He wasn't shy to admit it had all been by the hand of God. Two years prior, after his world had fallen apart following his parents' divorce, he'd renewed his faith. It had taken some time, but as each new store opened, the blessings multiplied.

"Derek, I'm happy you made it tonight." Ben Chadwick approached wearing a wide smile.

"Thank you for inviting me, Mr. Mayor." Derek extended his hand.

"Please, call me Ben. We're not into formalities in this town."

Derek relaxed a bit. He liked this man. "Ben it is."

"I'm happy to hear you've already been able to meet a few of our members. We have a great group of businesspeople who are always willing to exchange ideas and offer help. I know they're grateful you've agreed to speak tonight."

Speaking in front of a group had never been difficult for Derek. It was a trait he'd inherited from his father, although he'd rather not give him the credit. Derek had been honest with God about his struggle to forgive his father. It was wrong to carry that weight, but letting go of the pain his father had caused his family made forgiveness seem impossible.

"Look, there's your neighbor." Ben pointed across the room and waved a greeting.

Derek turned, and his eyes widened when he spotted Molly entering the library. She returned Ben's wave but tossed a look as cold as a frozen pond in Derek's direction. Despite the stink eye, she looked striking. Dressed in cream-colored pants with a matching turtleneck sweater, she turned several heads as she moved toward the refreshment table.

Derek watched as several townspeople approached Molly to say hello. The past burned in his mind. Would she ever be able to forgive him if she knew what he'd done the day of her wedding? Of course, Derek knew it was a lot to ask. He also knew that if he wanted to expand his franchise, he needed her to agree to accept his help. He strolled to the table to grab a cup of punch and stepped in line behind Molly.

"Good evening," he whispered.

Molly jumped. Splat. The serving ladle plunged into the porcelain bowl, sending red liquid flying in the air. "Oh no!" Molly looked down at her pants now covered with a crimson stain.

Frantic, Derek sprang into action. He snatched a handful of napkins at the end of the table and raced back to her. "I'm so sorry, Molly. I shouldn't have snuck up behind you." He passed her the napkins.

Molly's face reddened while she wiped her clothes. "It was my fault. I wasn't paying attention."

"I met George, the dry cleaner, earlier this evening. Please take your outfit to get it cleaned. I'll pay the bill." Why had he snuck up on her? Thanks to him, she'd be spending the rest of the night with stains on her once gorgeous outfit.

"I'm able to pay for my own cleaning." Molly tucked her chin low and avoided eye contact.

"Let him pay for it, Molly." Rusty poked his

head over Molly's shoulder. "I'm going to grab a seat."

Derek paused as the man scurried away with a cup of coffee cradled in his hands. "Financial struggles are nothing to be ashamed of, Molly." His gaze latched on to hers.

Molly squared her shoulders. "Who said I'm having money issues?"

A beat of silence ticked.

"My credit card machine."

"All right. Thank you." She flicked a glance toward Rusty, who'd settled into a front row seat.

Derek recalled Molly wincing earlier this morning when her payment was denied. His shoulders sank, remembering his conversation with Rusty. He was handling this delicate situation all wrong. "I wasn't implying you couldn't afford to have your clothes cleaned, Molly. It's just...your outfit looked so perfect. I feel bad I ruined it."

The grim expression she wore lightened. "I know you weren't." She turned her cautious emerald eyes toward him, and Derek's pulse quickened.

"The truth is, you're right. I feel as though I'm on a sinking ship, and the crew has handed out the last life preserver." She spun on her heel and dashed toward the restroom.

Derek kept his feet planted to the floor. His

heart told him to chase her down. To comfort her and tell her everything would be okay. But he couldn't. His heart had to stay out of the equation. In order to move forward with his well-charted plan, he had to keep his focus narrowed on the goal at hand. He needed to fulfill his promise and get Molly's store back in the black. And equally important, he needed to avoid emotional attachments at all cost.

Chapter Three

Molly squirmed in the cold metal folding chair. In the front of the room, Derek spoke to the crowd about his rise to fame in the business world. He fielded questions from the audience and was generous with his time. Molly had to admit, his speech was motivating, but even the aroma of the old library books around them failed to calm her nerves. Between the anticipation of admitting to her landlord she was almost broke and couldn't pay him what she owed, the sad looks Derek threw in her direction after she'd confessed she had no money, and the giant stain covering her expensive pants, she was ready to wave the white flag and call it a night.

The meeting dragged on longer than she'd expected—unlike her appointment at the bank earlier in the day. It had only taken ten minutes for the loan officer to let her know she didn't qualify for assistance, and that she was one late charge away from draining her checking account down to the last penny. Molly wasn't sure he'd needed to be that harsh. In the end, Molly transferred money from her emergency savings, but the account didn't have enough to cover last month's rent.

"Thank you for speaking to us tonight, Derek. Before we conclude for the evening, I have some big news to share," the mayor said. He gripped the sides of the podium at the front of the room and smiled. "Mountain Ridge Development, a major real estate developer from the Midwest, has its eye on Whispering Slopes and plans to make a trip to our town in the near future."

The group responded with a wave of chatter among themselves.

"What does it mean for us?" Ray Whitfield, one of two car mechanics in town, called out.

Molly wondered the same thing. Her gaze shot to Rusty, who appeared to hang on every word said. Was he picturing himself and his wife sipping lemonade with crushed ice while cruising the seas and enjoying life as retirees? Was the investor interested in his space as part of Mountain Ridge Development? Or was there even more interest? If Derek got a loan and out-bid everyone, could she trust the man who'd ruined her personal life with her career? As difficult as it was to admit, in order to save her business, she might need his help.

Ben Chadwick cleared his throat. "Since their visit is more of a scouting expedition, we don't know for sure what it could mean, but if they like what they see, it could result in a lot of positive economic growth for our area." He ruffled through the papers perched on top of the wooden podium.

Molly listened as the opposing opinions were flung around the room. Some folks were excited, while others wanted to keep the town as is. Rather than get upset about something that might never happen, she remained quiet. The discussion continued among the crowd, and the more she listened, the more she realized she couldn't deny the facts. There were already two people interested in purchasing Rusty's property, and one was in this room, continuing to throw glances in her direction.

Once the meeting concluded, Molly went in search of Rusty. Like ripping off a bandage, she was ready to get this conversation over and done with. *Great.* She bit her lower lip when she saw Rusty chatting with Derek. Thankfully, Rusty spotted her approaching and excused himself.

Relieved, she stood in place. She wasn't in the mood to deal with Derek for a second time tonight.

"I'm sorry to interrupt your conversation with Derek, but I'm anxious to get home tonight." She pushed a strand of flyaway hair from her face.

"No worries." Rusty glanced at his watch. "Do you want to go grab a quick cup of coffee?"

Molly shifted her weight from one foot to the other and shook her head. "I'm good. Listen, I've been worrying about this all day, so I'm going to come out and say it."

Rusty placed his hand on Molly's arm. "You need more time for the rent, right? It's okay."

Boy, talk about a hard pill to swallow. One of her oldest and dearest friends in Whispering Slopes didn't have confidence in her ability to operate a successful business, but she couldn't blame him. "I'm sorry, Rusty. I thought I'd be in a position to pay you by now. I had a meeting at the bank, but it didn't go so well." Her chin trembled. She felt like a complete failure. "I hope this won't have any bearing on your decision to sell sooner. I just need more time."

"I told you and Derek I'm willing to wait, but I can't hold off forever. I'll give you the thirty days. Who knows, maybe I won't feel pressured to sell if your store is doing better by then. In the meantime, you'll pay me when you can. But I am concerned about anyone other than myself you might owe money to. I know it's none of my business, but I promised your mother I'd look after you."

A long silence stretched.

Molly would give anything to have her mother here to confess her troubles to. She'd always been such a good listener. A cup of her chamomile tea and unconditional love were the best medicine. "I know you gave her your word, Rusty. I appreciate it. I do. But I'll be fine."

"Please remember to pay everyone else first. I don't want you to jeopardize your credit score."

Molly gave Rusty a quick peck on the cheek. "I won't. I've got to go. Thank you again for everything."

Outside in the parking lot, Molly breathed in the cool evening air scented with fresh pine. She loved autumn in the Shenandoah Valley.

Molly climbed into her car and secured the seat belt. Her shoulders slumped. Would her financial situation prevent her from making a home for Grace? She released a heavy sigh, and a thickness formed in her throat. She turned on the ignition and headed home to an empty house and to another night alone.

* * *

The next morning, Molly dusted off the last shelf in the store and moved to the back office to prioritize the invoices she'd disregarded yesterday. With a list of tasks a mile long, she was excited to prepare for the upcoming Book Buddies meeting.

She was startled by a knock at the front door and examined her watch. Who would be shopping for books at seven o'clock? She pushed away from her desk, smoothed her hair and headed to the front. Like a tractor trailer hitting the brakes for a railroad crossing, Molly stopped. Through the glass, she saw Derek wearing a dark leather jacket and holding two cups of coffee. The caffeine was welcome, but his company wasn't.

With Derek working next door, she'd realized they'd bump into each other more often than she'd like. What she hadn't expected was for him to come knocking at her door before business hours. Oh right, he was helping his poor, penniless neighbor by providing a free caffeine fix. She unlocked the entrance.

"Good morning," he sang out and passed her the cup. "I thought I'd get your day started with one of my new drinks. I need someone to sample it before I present it to the public. Would you mind?"

"So you want me to be your guinea pig?" Molly ran the beverage underneath her nose. She had to admit, the aroma was enticing. "It smells so yummy. What is it?"

Molly watched as Derek removed his coat and hung it over his muscular arm. Did he plan to stay? She had more important things to accomplish, and on top of her list was to keep as far away from Derek McKinney as possible.

"It's a snickerdoodle latte." He sipped, made a slurping sound and followed it with a boyish grin.

Molly stifled a giggle.

"Sorry. Try it. I've been experimenting with some new recipes this morning."

Molly took a drink. The flavors exploded in her mouth like she was sinking her teeth into a hot, syrupy cinnamon roll, fresh out of the oven. "Mmm...this is the best latte I've ever tasted. I'm serious." No wonder this guy had customers swarming his store. She licked the creamy froth from her upper lip. "Is that caramel I taste?"

"Yes, but only a dollop. It's not too much, is it?"

She shook her head and took another sip. "Oh no. It's perfect. If I knew this was waiting for me each morning, I'd spring out of bed without ever hitting the snooze button."

Derek laughed. "Well, feel free to pay me a visit anytime. I'll have it ready for you. Or I can hand-deliver it, if you prefer." He winked.

Was he flirting with her? No. He couldn't be. Whatever his intentions, she needed him to leave. She felt light-headed. "Well, thanks again for the coffee. I need to get back to work."

"It's not even seven thirty. I hoped we could visit for a while. You know, talk shop." He strolled toward one of the tables with two club chairs. Pulling out a seat, he motioned for her to sit down. "Please, let's relax and enjoy our coffee. I like to ease into my day."

With a daunting list of things to do, Molly had no time for small talk. This was not what she'd expected when she'd arrived at the store earlier. He was the reason she'd been left at the altar. Kicking back and sipping a latte with him wasn't on her schedule. "I don't mean to be rude, but I don't have time for this."

"Please, sit. Just for a couple of minutes."

Against her better judgment, she plopped down in the seat. Determined not to lose herself in his handsome good looks, she kept her eyes on the hairline crack on the brown wall behind him.

Derek took a seat, folded his hands and rested

them on the table. "Let me guess. You're one of those people who schedules everything—even a coffee break."

"Is there something wrong with taking control of your day?" Molly took pride in her excellent time management skills. She found pleasure in checking things off her to-do list each day. Sometimes she would write down tasks she had already accomplished if only for the satisfaction of making a red check mark.

"No, but you need to have some downtime. You know...to enjoy life." He leaned back in the chair and clasped his hands around the back of his head.

"Not all of us have the luxury to sit back while the money rolls in." Molly couldn't remember the last time she'd had a day off.

Derek's brow arched. "So you think I don't work hard?"

Heat prickled her face. "No. I'm sorry. I guess I assumed since you're so successful, you have other people doing the work for you."

"I'll let you in on a secret. The more successful you are, the busier you become." He half smiled. "But it all comes down to time management."

Molly released a heavy sigh, and her body went limp. "How is it I can be so busy but not generate a profit?" The minute she said it, she wanted to take it back. He was the last person she wanted to discuss her dire financial situation with. But he was known in the business world. At least, that was what she'd heard from others in the community. Since she couldn't get a loan, he might be her last hope at keeping her shop.

Derek studied her before speaking again. "Can I ask you something?"

"Well, I guess it depends." She wiggled in her chair and wished she hadn't decided to come in early this morning.

"I know the big chain bookstore has had an impact on your sales. How bad is it?"

Molly was unable to make eye contact, and she wished she'd never confessed her financial woes. The last thing she wanted was pity—especially from Derek.

"Look, it's nothing to be ashamed of. Big chain stores have been swallowing mom-and-pop shops for years."

"Well, that doesn't sound encouraging," she croaked.

"I didn't mean to sound so pessimistic. I want you to know your financial struggles are not all your fault. You've got some tough competition, but I can help you."

"With Rusty wanting to sell, I don't know what's going to happen." A lump started to form in Molly's throat. It was only a matter of time before the tears would follow. "I need to get back to work. Thank you for the coffee. People will love it."

"I'm sorry, Molly. I shouldn't have said anything. Look, I know people are funny about money. It's not something most are comfortable talking about, but ignoring the facts could have major repercussions for your business."

Molly knew her business was failing, and if she didn't do something soon, she'd have to close the doors. With no income, how could she proceed with the adoption process? What would happen to Grace? She needed advice, but why did the one person who could save her bookstore have to be Derek McKinney?

Unsure what to say, Derek remained silent as Molly dried her tears. Was her financial situation worse than Rusty had disclosed? Did he know how serious the situation had become? As Derek scanned her store, he saw the potential. Sure, the big chain stores might offer discounts to entice shoppers, but Molly could give her customers so much more. From the moment he'd walked inside, it smelled of books with a hint of freshly cut lemons. The atmosphere in her shop was warm and welcoming.

"With a few changes, your store could be what shoppers escaping the city for a peaceful visit in the mountains would love. Why would they go to the big-name bookstore when they're on vacation? They could do that at home." The more time he spent inside Molly's shop, the more he realized this place was a hidden gem.

"I'm sorry. I didn't mean to have a complete meltdown." Using her fingers, she blotted her eyes. "It's hard to lose something that's been your dream for so long."

Derek chewed his lower lip in an attempt to silence the thoughts racing through his mind. Thanks to him, Molly had already lost one desire. Most little girls dreamed of getting married and raising a family. How could he allow her to suffer disappointment a second time? "You have to fight for it. You don't have to lose anything. Let me help you."

"Why would you want to do that? You've got a new store you're getting off the ground. I know how much work goes into an opening. Besides, what makes you think I'd want your help? In the past, you weren't my number one fan."

Point taken. "Look, I know we were never great friends."

Molly huffed. "You can say that again."

How could he convince her? The potential he saw for his own business in Whispering Slopes was too great to walk away from. If he could help Molly succeed, he'd have the opportunity to get some prime real estate at a great price. But it was equally important for him to keep his promise to Rusty. Going back on his word wasn't an option. He wasn't like his father, a man who'd made his own son and wife feel like they weren't enough. "Rusty isn't going to make any major decisions anytime soon. Give me at least the same amount of time Rusty is allowing. It's all I ask. I won't make any more surprise visits to your store. If I don't increase your sales and get your store turning over a steady profit, you can continue to despise me and pretend I don't exist."

Molly pulled the cuffs of her angora sweater over her hands and crossed her arms. "Why would you believe I despise you?"

Derek shrugged his tense shoulders. He didn't know if Ryan had mentioned his name when he called off the wedding. "Just a hunch, I guess."

"So why do you want to help me? Especially

if you think I don't like you." Her eyebrows peaked.

"At the risk of sounding too confident, I'm good at helping struggling business owners. I can turn a business around and make it successful." He paused and looked around the room. "Consider what you have here. It's not just a room full of books, Molly. I see real potential. By implementing some new marketing strategies, your store could be a big success. I mean it."

Her eyes sparkled with a glint of hopefulness. "You think so? I guess all I see is a dream I worked countless hours to build slipping away."

Molly flinched when the store phone behind the counter rang. "Excuse me for one second." She pushed herself away from the table. Next to the telephone was a box of tissues. He watched as she snatched one and wiped her eyes before answering.

Derek sipped the latte, which had gotten cold. It still tasted pretty good to him. He observed the books lining the shelves and looked down at his cup. Offering a free specialty coffee to anyone who had a receipt from a book purchased at her store might help to boost her sales. Would she go for his idea? Rusty was right about her. The woman was stubborn. She liked to do things on her own. It was an admirable trait, and he had his work cut out for him if he hoped to convince Molly he could help.

Molly's phone conversation ended and she returned to the table. She took a seat and looked more distraught than when she'd left. How was that possible?

"What's wrong?" Derek leaned toward her.

"The teacher who planned to bring the children over next Wednesday for Book Buddies, my book club, has canceled." Her eyelashes fluttered as tears brimmed the lids.

"Did she say why?"

Molly nodded. "Something about having to go out of town and she can't find a replacement."

"I'm sorry, but they'll come the next time." Derek wasn't quite sure why the phone call had sparked such a reaction. Did Molly think there might not be a next time for her club or for her store? "It's not the end of the world," he said, hoping to sound encouraging.

"You don't understand. On the days the kids are here, I have some of my best sales, since the kids come in with parents or other family members. They browse while the children and I discuss the book. They often make purchases before they leave. We already missed this week because of a teachers' workday." She covered her eyes and wept.

This was worse than he'd thought. Derek wasn't sure how to respond, so he sat in silence.

After the last whimper, Molly removed her hands from her face. "I'll never be able to pay Rusty the money I owe him." She paused, and her eyes glazed over with fear. "Or the pile of bills multiplying each day. I'm going to lose everything."

Derek reached across the table and covered her hand with his. "You need to trust me, Molly. Please, let me help you. I know how to generate a profit." Derek would never forget how incredible it had felt to tally the sales for the year from his first store. He had a head for business and had found his calling. The four years he had studied marketing in college had paid off. Each store he bought had turned into a moneymaker. Could this be the way to make things right with Molly?

Molly remained silent. Would she refuse his offer and decide to handle the problem on her own? If she failed, they both failed. Rusty would sell to the developers, and both of their businesses could become office space. Derek had no doubt he could help Molly, and then he'd be able to get the space for the lower price. But she would need to put their past behind them. He watched as she glanced around the bookstore before turning back to him, her face void of expression. "This is all I have. Please help me, Derek."

Chapter Four

Molly shelved the last book from the shipment that had arrived after Derek left her store. She tilted her head from side to side in an attempt to work out the kinks in her neck. She glanced at her watch, and her stomach twisted. Why had she spilled her heart to Derek? What was she thinking asking him for help with the bookstore? After her total and complete meltdown in front of him earlier, he'd suggested they go on a field trip this evening. Feeling desperate, she'd agreed. Was she a glutton for punishment? From the moment he returned to his shop, she'd second-guessed her decision.

"Is there anything else you need before I head out to class, Molly?"

Caitlin Dickerson, a high-energy college student who had worked part-time for Molly since last year, breezed in from the back room. Unable to afford a full-time employee, Molly had sought assistance through the local community college and received a major blessing when they recommended Caitlin. She was enrolled in a work-study program offered by the school and earning credit toward her degree, so Molly didn't have to pay her a salary. The girl loved books and was a hard worker. It was the perfect combination. Caitlin reminded Molly of herself in her late teens. Molly couldn't devour books fast enough. Of course, once she got bit by the writing bug, she had to cut back to one book a week.

"You've done more than enough today. Thank you so much for completing the inventory. It's a huge load off of my plate. You did a great job."

Caitlin beamed. "You're welcome. Working here is the best part of my day."

The front door chimed, and both women turned.

"Wow," Caitlin leaned in and whispered to Molly. "Bookworms are getting better-looking."

Derek. Molly's stomach went into a double knot.

"He's our new neighbor," Molly responded.

"Good evening, ladies." Derek sauntered toward the back of the store, commanding Caitlin's full attention. Molly wasn't surprised. In college, when Derek entered the classroom, female necks stretched like elastic bands. He still had that power.

Molly managed to find her voice. "Derek, this is Caitlin Dickerson. She's an employee here at the store." Of course, soon he would discover Caitlin was her only employee. Molly had hoped to have several employees, people who shared her love of books, but she could hardly pay herself, much less a staff.

"It's a pleasure to meet you, Caitlin." Derek extended his hand.

"You're the coffee mogul." Caitlin's cheeks reddened.

Molly considered her assistant. How had she heard of Derek and his success?

Caitlin pivoted to Molly. "We studied Mr. McKinney in my marketing class last semester."

"Please, call me Derek."

"You're a great example of how hard work and dedication pay off." Caitlin paused for a moment. "You're famous in my class."

Molly's brow rocketed into an arch at her employee's statement. Famous? Really?

"My professor has lectured about your business plan. Most of my classmates have dreams to open businesses of their own. You're a real inspiration."

Derek listened as Caitlin continued to sing his praises. Molly fought the urge to roll her eyes, but Caitlin sounded sincere.

When the young girl stopped to catch a breath, her eyes widened. "Maybe you could speak to our class?"

"I've spoken at several schools in the state. I'd be honored to visit yours, if invited."

"You would? That's so cool! I'll send my professor a text message. He'll be thrilled." Caitlin snatched her canvas book bag from the counter and flung it over her shoulder. "It was great to meet you, Mr.— Sorry, Derek. Thank you again for your generous offer. I'll come by your shop once I hear from my instructor. See you tomorrow, Molly."

"Thanks again for your help today, Caitlin." Molly watched as Caitlin floated out of the store. She turned to Derek. "Are you sure you have time to speak at Caitlin's school? You're just getting your new place up and running."

"I always make time for young and motivated entrepreneurs. My success can be credited to a mentor in the restaurant business. He gave his time and advice freely, so I try to do the same when I can." A silence lingered before Derek spoke again. "Are you ready to head out?"

Molly had no idea what he had planned, but

if it would help save the bookstore, she couldn't allow their past to get in the way. She straightened her shoulders. *Grow up, girl. This is your business. Put your feelings aside and go along.* "So, will you tell me where we're going?"

"Lock up and grab your purse. You'll find out soon enough," Derek said, flashing a smile that had always made Molly's college classmates swoon. But not her. Never.

Thirty minutes later, Derek navigated his SUV into the strip mall parking lot. Molly's jaw tightened when she peered out the window. The large glowing green lights of her competitor's sign taunted her. "Why did you bring me here?"

"As a business owner, it's always a good idea to check out your competition." Derek winked before he unfastened his seat belt.

Molly followed his lead. They stepped from the vehicle, and Molly turned to Derek. "I've been in stores like this millions of times." Before opening Bound to Please Reads, she'd loved traveling to neighboring towns and visiting bookstores. She'd peruse the aisles with a coffee in hand before curling up in a comfy chair to work on her novel.

"True, but you visited as a customer, not as a business owner."

Molly scratched the back of her head. "I don't understand why it would make any difference."

Derek nodded in the direction of the store. "Let's go inside. I'll show you."

The moment they entered the store responsible for slowing her sales, the aroma of freshly brewed coffee teased Molly's nose. Her heart sank as she took in the surroundings. "It's so crowded in here." She hadn't meant to say it out loud. The customers buzzed around and scanned the end displays that held the most recent bestsellers. Giant colorful posters covered the walls. She hung her head. How could she ever compete with such a successful business model?

"What better way to spend a Friday night than hanging out in a bookstore?" Derek commented.

Molly moved with caution across the tiled floor. The clicking of fingers on a keyboard from a nearby laptop caught her attention. She turned to see a young woman. Was she a published author or working on her first manuscript? At the end of the same oak table, an older man with wire-framed glasses paged through a magazine.

"Besides your children's book club, do people ever come into your store to write or hang out and read?" Derek asked in a low voice.

Molly shook her head. "I've thought about starting an adult book club or teaching a writing class, but there never seems to be enough time." Tucked inside the pages of her brown leather journal, Molly had an endless list of things she wanted to do both personally and professionally.

Derek's brow arched. "You write? Have you ever been published?"

Prior to selling her first short story to a magazine, the question had always made Molly cringe. She used to wonder if you had to be published to be a writer. Writers wrote—right? It's what they did whether they were published or not. "Yes, I sold a few short stories, but now I'm writing a novel."

"Wow. A book? Impressive. You should consider hosting workshops at your store. If you did it one or two evenings a month, it would bring people into the shop." Derek pointed around the oversized space. "Look at all of the people working on their computers. I'm sure if you asked, more than half are aspiring novelists."

"But they're here to write, not buy books."

"You're promoting traffic. Getting people in the door is half the battle of running a business, because once they are inside, you've got them in the palm of your hand." He spoke with a devious tone and rubbed his hands together.

Molly giggled. "You sound like a spider who caught a giant fly in its web."

"It's a perfect analogy. Of course, I wouldn't expect any less from a wordsmith like yourself." Derek grinned. "So, what first captured your attention when you walked into the store? Apart from the crowds," he added.

Nearby, a young girl cheered. Gleaming with pride, she proclaimed to her mother she'd found the book she'd been looking for. Molly smiled. She longed to share such a moment with her own child. She turned and pointed toward the right side of the store. "Besides the smell of coffee, the author doing a book signing and the enormous free-standing sign with his book cover. It's the first thing I noticed." Having an event like this for her own book was a dream for her, but the road to publication felt far away.

"You could do that."

Molly crossed her arms. "Well, first I need to finish the book. After that comes the daunting task of querying agents. Hopefully, they can sell it to a publisher. I'm not sure I have the stamina or the tough skin for all of the rejections."

Derek laughed. "I meant you could host author meet and greets at your shop."

"Oh right." Molly's face flushed with warmth. Her own book signing? How could it ever happen when she hadn't added to her word count in days? The well was dry with the mountain of bills she had to pay. "I've had a couple authors come in for signings, but the events never seem to have a significant impact on sales."

"Maybe you need to get a bigger name to commit. Or perhaps you didn't do enough advertising to promote the event. As for getting your novel published, I'd argue against you not having the stamina."

Uncertainty rattled her core. "These days, I don't have the time to work on my book. If business doesn't improve, Rusty will sell, and I could lose everything I have worked so hard for. That's kind of squashed my creativity."

Derek reached out and placed his hand over hers. "I won't let that happen. I promise you."

With a past flooded by a sea of broken promises, Molly struggled with his words. She skimmed the room and focused back on Derek. Trusting didn't come easy for her. They were spending time together to save her store and pay off debt. With the Lord's help, she would welcome Grace into her home. Those were her priorities. She refused to allow empty promises to override logic. She sucked in a deep breath and exhaled. Not this time.

* * *

Derek tried to keep his focus on the matter at hand. Keeping Molly's store open was important to his own success, but the floral scent wafting from her direction made his thoughts jumbled and fuzzy. Why did she have to smell so good? But it wasn't only her alluring scent. Tonight, her shiny red hair was pulled back with a black clip, and loose tendrils framed her face. He struggled to keep his eyes off her. Distance. It's what he needed. He sidestepped her in the direction of the children's section of the bookstore.

"Look over there." Derek pointed toward the small wooden rocking chairs painted bright red. They'd been placed in a semicircle in front of an adult-sized rocking chair.

"Oh, how sweet. I'd love to have those in my store." Molly clasped her hands together and pressed them against her chest.

A large and colorful sign to the left of the reading area advertised story time on Saturday afternoons at three o'clock. "See." Derek nodded toward the sign. "You could do the same. It's a terrific way to get the entire family into the store on what should be your most profitable day of the week."

"I'm not sure I could ever draw a crowd like this store." Molly sighed.

Derek had a hard time relating to Molly's defeated attitude. When it came to his businesses, he knew having a positive mindset was a must. On the other hand, he had never been in her position. This was going to be more difficult than he'd thought. "Of course you could. You have one thing this place can never have."

"What?"

It was the reason Derek had decided to tweak his business model away from larger cities. "A small town with a welcoming atmosphere. People love to escape the hectic rat race and head to the mountains."

"But I'm one person. How can I offer writing classes, host Book Buddies and author signings, and assist customers?"

This was a problem, but not one without a solution. When it came to business, Derek believed every difficulty could be overcome, but he did wonder how Molly was able to meet payroll. "Look, I don't want to pry, but if I'm going to help you, I need to know the details. How are you able to pay Caitlin?"

Molly's gaze skimmed the floor before she turned to him. "Caitlin volunteers her time. I found her through the community college. She's earning her degree in literature and obtains credit for her time at my store."

Impressive. Molly had a better head for business than she gave herself credit for. "That's genius."

Her face flushed. "Well, I'm not so sure... but thanks."

"Let's grab a cup of coffee and have a seat over there." Derek pointed to a quiet table for two on the other side of the store.

Moments later, with steaming cups of brew in hand, Derek pulled out the chair for Molly. He settled into his seat, placed a leather portfolio on the table, opened it to a blank sheet of paper and removed the pen from its holder. He was almost never without paper and something to write with. Sure, he could jot notes or record his thoughts on his phone, but this was the way he had documented some of his greatest business ideas, so why change?

Molly smiled. "I thought I was the only person left on earth who uses paper and pen. I'm a bit of a hoarder when it comes to journals."

Did they have more in common than he'd realized? He had drawers overflowing with notebooks waiting to be filled with the next great idea. "I thought we could make a list of some changes you can implement to generate a profit." Derek wrote fast. "The first thing is to expand on something you're already doing."

"You mean I'm doing something right?" Molly shook her head and laughed.

"You're too hard on yourself. You're doing a lot of things right. You've got good business sense, but you need to do it on a bigger scale. What I said earlier about utilizing Caitlin being a great idea is true. She helps you, but you're helping her and your community. That's smart. You need to give yourself more credit."

"I guess it's hard to stay positive when you see your dream vanishing."

Derek placed the pen on the table. "If you want to do this, you'll have to keep your focus and remain confident."

"It was always easy for you, wasn't it?"

"Keeping my focus?"

Molly leaned back against the cushioned chair. "Well, that and maintaining a confident attitude. I remember you had an air about you in college. People gravitated to you." She lifted the foam cup, took a sip of the beverage and placed it on the table. "I suppose it's what happens when a child is raised in a loving environment."

Molly's words rattled Derek to the core. They couldn't be further from the truth. But once upon a time, he'd believed the same.

Pools of sadness consumed her eyes, a reminder of what he had done to her in the past. A quick change of topic was in order.

"So, what did you mean about a bigger

scale?" Her question sent a message. She was also ready to change the conversation. Relieved, he reached for the pen and tapped it against the page.

"You should reach out to the college again. I'm sure there are more students like Caitlin. It might be too late in the semester for them to gain credit, but the work experience would be invaluable. With additional help, you'll have free time to get more personal with the customers and offer more events. Best of all, it won't eat into your budget. It's a win-win situation."

"I can do that. In fact, I think Caitlin mentioned she has a classmate who's interested."

"Perfect." Derek recorded additional notes.

"What's next on your list?" Molly's lips parted into a half smile. For the first time this evening, concern lifted from her face.

"I thought we could partner up to generate more sales for you. I can give my customers a discount toward a purchase at my coffee shop if they provide a receipt from your store. But their purchase would need to be on a full-price item. None of those books from your discount table."

Molly straightened her shoulders. She might be interested in his advice to save her store, but he got the sense she wasn't on board with this idea.

"So you don't think I can do it on my own?"

Her brow steepled. "Why would I accept charity from you of all people?"

Good point. Molly shouldn't want his help, especially if she believed he had something to do with ruining what should have been the most special day of her life. How could he blame her? He needed a different strategy to convince her. "Hey, it's not charity. I'm looking after myself, too."

"How can the offer help you?" Her eyes reflected doubt. She didn't trust him.

"People have a tendency to buy more if they believe they are getting something for free. It's human nature. By me offering them the credit, I'll generate more sales, so it's all a wash."

Molly leaned forward, placing her elbows on the table. "A wash, huh?"

She wasn't buying it. "Have you noticed the price of gourmet coffee these days? The stuff isn't cheap, but people love it. I think they deserve something for the dent I'm making in their wallets. Besides, books and coffee just go together." He scribbled some additional details on the paper, hoping to move on.

"Do you think these little things can save my bookstore? I know you're brilliant when it comes to coffee sales, but books aren't the same."

"Sales are sales. It all comes down to branding and marketing. And yes, I do think implementing some of these changes will help, but it won't put you back into positive territory—"

"So what's the point?" Molly interrupted.

"You didn't let me finish."

"Sorry." She cupped her hand over her mouth.

"What I was saying is you need to do more—a lot more. And the first thing is a store makeover."

Molly giggled. "Sorry, but what do you know about makeovers?"

"I'm not talking about makeup." He chuckled. "I mean a complete staging. We create an atmosphere guaranteed to attract customers. One that will make them feel as though they are in their own home."

"But that costs money. I'm not flush with cash at the moment."

Derek had already spoken with Rusty about his idea, and their landlord had given the green light to making some improvements. A last-ditch effort to help Molly. "Fortunately, our landlord knows the importance of keeping his properties well-maintained. It's been a number of years since he's given the walls a fresh coat of paint."

A sparkle flashed in Molly's eyes. "Those brown walls are drab, aren't they? I always thought a warm shade of blue would be nice."

Derek nodded. "Now you're thinking. Studies show people respond well to the color blue. It makes them feel you're trustworthy."

"So, when do we start?"

The excitement in Molly's voice was something he'd been waiting for. If they were going to turn her business around, he needed her to be enthusiastic about the project. "That's what I wanted to hear. Since the store is closed on Sunday, which is something else we need to address, we could start—"

"What do you mean? What is there to address?"

Derek understood why some businesses preferred not to open on Sunday. It was the day of Lord, and a day people liked to rest. The problem was, if she wanted to compete with the big guys, remaining open seven days a week was a must. "I think you need to keep the shop open on Sunday—at least for a while."

"You mean until I get enough money to pay my rent, everyone I owe, plus the overhead."

He sensed the defeat again in Molly's tone. "If you think about it, you're missing out on those customers who are in town for their weekend mountain getaway." Derek planned to keep his store open in order to cater to the leaf peepers who flocked to the mountains this time of year. "Autumn is the perfect time to test your Sunday traffic. In a couple of weeks, the foliage will peak."

"As much as I hate to admit it, I think you're right. I have had an uptick in business during the autumn months."

Considering their past, agreeing with him wasn't easy for her. He understood that. "I think we should close the store on Monday and get the painting done during the week. We don't want to lose your Saturday traffic, so we could start the job after you close tomorrow and then finish on Monday. I know this isn't the best time to shut down your business, but if we're going to do this makeover, painting should be our first task. Going forward, we can test staying open on Sunday. We'll monitor your sales to see if it's a profitable business decision. We could have your hours set from noon until four o'clock."

Molly remained quiet. A store employee skirted their table. A scanner from a front register beeped. Was this too much for her? Or was the problem that it was him offering the help? "What do you say?"

She cleared her throat. "But what about your store? Don't you need to tend to your own business?"

"I have two new hires starting tomorrow. Both have barista experience, so I'll spend a few hours with them, but they should be fine to cover things. Besides, I'll be next door, so I can keep an eye on them."

"Okay. Let's start the job tomorrow evening." Molly grabbed her cup. "I'm going to stop at the restroom before we go." She pushed herself away from the table, tossed her beverage into a nearby trash can and headed toward the back of the store.

Could she move any faster? It was apparent Molly couldn't wait to get away from him. Derek sucked in a steadying breath and raked his fingers through his hair. He wouldn't allow Molly's store to fail. He'd given Rusty his word. Of course, spending so much time together wasn't going to be easy.

Chapter Five

Late Saturday afternoon, Molly flipped the sign to Closed. Her shoulders drooped. Another day of lackluster book sales. If things didn't pick up soon, the shop would sink faster than a penny tossed into a fountain. Earlier, she'd received a text message from the teacher who administered the Book Buddies group for the schools. She'd arranged for another class to come to Molly's store. At least that was some encouraging news. *Stay positive.* That was Molly's latest mantra.

Mindlessly moving through the store, she struggled to keep her focus. A quick glance at her watch told her why. Derek would be here within the next fifteen minutes. Last night, after returning home from her field trip with Derek, she'd spiraled down the rabbit hole of online browsing. She'd finally made a decision on the paint color for the shop and emailed Derek the information. His response had been instant. He'd offered to pick up the paint today and come by after closing to start the project. Why did he have to be so obliging? Perhaps he was a man with a guilty conscience?

Moments later, Molly turned to the sound of someone pecking on the glass. She moved toward the door, spotted Annie peeking through the window and motioned her to come inside.

"I'm sorry. I didn't think you'd be closed this early." Annie gazed around the shop.

"I'm not usually, but I'm getting ready to do some interior painting. You know, brighten the place up a bit."

Annie smiled. "That will be nice. Maybe Grace can help you? I thought you might like to spend some more time with her."

A warmth filled Molly's heart at the mention of her name. "Of course, I'd love that." Then she remembered Derek. "The store owner from next door has offered to help and will be here."

"Oh, Derek McKinney. I've met him already. He seems like a great guy. Well, then you could have two extra sets of hands," Annie suggested. "I can bring Grace by tomorrow morning, if that's okay? Does nine o'clock work?"

Molly would prefer to spend time alone with Grace, but she wasn't going to pass up an opportunity to see that sweet little face again. "That would be wonderful."

"Great. I'll see you tomorrow." Annie gave Molly a quick hug before leaving the store.

She hadn't planned on sharing her plans to adopt with Derek, but since they'd be spending time together, he'd find out soon enough. Besides, there was no such thing as a secret in Whispering Slopes.

Moments later, another knock sounded. It was time to get to work. Derek stood outside the door dressed in relaxed-fit jeans and a black sweatshirt dotted with white paint splatters.

She opened the door and caught a trace of his woodsy scent. "Hello." She tried to tell herself the smell wasn't all that pleasant, but who was she kidding? She loved to take long hikes in the woods and brainstorm her novel. Why did this man make her brain feel like an overripe banana? "Please, come in." She forced a smile.

"I would have been here sooner, but Caitlin stopped by to see me." Derek worked his way across the room with a large can of paint in each hand. An oversized backpack hung from his right shoulder. He placed the supplies on the counter and turned. "She got the okay from her professor. It looks like I'll be speaking to her marketing class."

A twinge of guilt rattled her. No matter how

she felt about Derek, it was generous of him to offer his time to the college students. He already had a full plate with his store and helping her. "I'm sure they'll be excited for your visit."

"I'm looking forward to it, too. I love to see students excited to learn about the business world."

Molly hoped their bubbles didn't burst like hers. Well, hers was more of a slow leak. "Make sure you don't sugarcoat it. Business can be brutal." She had the battle scars to prove it.

"Come on, Mols."

Molly's brow crinkled. Mols? Since when did he have a nickname for her? That's what friends did, and he wasn't a friend. Derek was a successful businessman offering his advice. That was all. "What?"

"You've just hit a rough patch."

Easy for him to say. He had seven or eight coffee shops. Plus, he came from money. If he ever struggled, he'd probably run to his family for cash.

"Why the silent treatment?"

"This is much more than a rough patch, as you call it. This is my livelihood. I don't have a rich daddy to run to when things get difficult." She bit hard on her lower lip. When would she learn not to say the first thought that popped into her head?

Derek remained quiet, but his shoulders were rigid. She'd hit a nerve.

"I'm sorry. I was out of line." This would be a long night if she didn't turn this conversation in a different direction. It wasn't the time to dig up the past. And why would she want to? It was best to keep it buried along with her feelings.

"No, you don't." He pulled a screwdriver from his back pocket and began to pry open the can of paint. "My family isn't open for discussion."

Her stomach clenched into a tight ball. He meant business. His tone spoke volumes, but his eyes expressed sadness.

She stepped closer to the counter. "Understood. I'm sorry. So, what do you think of the paint color I selected?"

Derek peered at it. "I think it will look great." He removed the lid from the can and unzipped his bag.

Relieved to see Derek had moved on from her remarks, she still couldn't help but wonder about his reaction. In college, Derek's family life had appeared perfect on the outside. *Like your store seems perfect to outsiders.* Maybe his life wasn't so flawless. Molly's eye went toward the unopened container of paint. "Wait. What's with the yellow?" She reached out and slid the product closer.

Derek removed a wooden stirrer from the bag and plunged it into the thick blue paint. "Remember the children's section at the bookstore last night?"

She did. In fact, after their visit to her competition, her mind had been flooded with dreams of a colorful house filled with children who were all loved, not brought into a home just for the money. *If it weren't for you, I couldn't buy this beer.* No. She shook away the hateful words that had stolen her childhood. "Yes, it was wonderful."

With one last stir, Derek let go of the stick and ran his hands down the sides of his jeans. "I think this area over here would be a perfect spot to incorporate a children's area." He moved toward the side of the store.

From the moment Rusty had shown Molly the empty space, she'd known it would be the perfect location to open her bookstore. She'd been drawn to the area where Derek stood. The small alcove had floor-to-ceiling windows that looked out onto a landscaped courtyard with a fountain. She had dreamed of doing something special with the space but had never been quite sure what to do. Until now. Why hadn't she thought of it?

"What do you think?" He turned with his arms extended.

She scanned the area that held a table display of a few bestsellers, along with some classics. It was drab and not the least bit appealing with the walls painted brown. Why hadn't she thought to talk Rusty out of picking the color? But at the time Rusty had last painted, she'd still been mourning the loss of her mother. Her mind had been in a dark place. "I love the idea."

"It's a great space. It brings the outdoors inside."

Molly's mouth dropped open. He'd hit the nail on the head. "You're right. It's why I love it so much."

"I thought we could paint this back wall yellow." He pointed to the area alongside the windows. "We could get those tiny rocking chairs and paint some blue and others yellow. In addition, we could put in some built-in bookcases. That large table takes up a lot of space."

The sound of an empty cash register ringing permeated Molly's ears. "But it all costs money. Rusty might have agreed to pay for some paint, but I'm not sure about all these extra expenses."

"Don't worry. It's covered." He pivoted in the opposite direction.

Wait. Who was covering it? Was this another act of charity from Derek? Or was Rusty footing the bill? "Can I ask who's paying for this?

I'll need to know so I can repay them." At least, she hoped she could.

"I've cleared it with Rusty, since he still owns the property. We got the green light since it'll add value to the space. Of course, if we don't get started soon, you'll never be able to reopen by Tuesday. Greg, the handyman, should be here any minute to install some additional bookshelves. Rusty gave me his name. He comes highly recommended."

Molly was impressed. No wonder Derek was such a success. This guy gave new meaning to not allowing the grass to grow under your feet. "What do you want me to do?"

Derek glanced out the window. "We'll get started on painting the other parts of the store while Greg works over here. Since our time is limited, we'll have to work fast. I hope you brought a change of clothes." His gaze skimmed her from head to toe. "Your outfit is too pretty to be slopping around with paint."

Her cheeks warmed with the compliment. "It looks like you've already done some painting yourself." She playfully poked the front of his sweatshirt.

Derek chuckled and yanked on the bottom of his shirt. "Yeah, I did some painting in my office this morning. It needed a fresh look."

Molly moved in for closer examination. "Ecru?"

"Close. It's eggshell."

"So you went to the paint store, painted, and ran your coffee shop today?"

"Remember, I hired the baristas. There won't be a need to micromanage them. They started today, and they've already taken over the place. The customers love them."

"Are they students?" Molly longed for a day she could have full-time employees so she could focus more on her writing. Her stomach twisted. Would there even be a future for her store?

"Actually, they are seniors."

"High school?"

Derek laughed. "No. They are senior citizens—Charles and Nell. They're fantastic. It turns out they used to run their own shop in West Virginia. They sold their successful business when they retired, but after a year of traveling, they missed the coffee industry. After they moved to Whispering Slopes, they considered opening a new store, but they saw my ad and agreed it's perfect for them. They can have the fun and daily interactions with regular customers without the headaches that go along with owning a business."

Molly knew all about those headaches. In the past couple of months, she'd taken more aspirin than she could ever remember taking. "They sound like the perfect fit. Let me run and change so we can get started."

Seconds later, while back in her office, she heard the bell over the front door chime. She should have locked it after Derek arrived, but if it was a customer, she didn't want to miss out on a sale. She changed her outfit in record time.

Molly stepped from her office and her eyes widened. Annie stood talking with Derek.

"Hey, Molly."

Molly approached and spied a pocket folder clutched in the social worker's arms. Her heart pounded against her rib cage. She hadn't had an opportunity to tell Derek about Grace. "Annie, I'm surprised to see you again."

"I completely forgot to give this to you when I stopped by earlier." Annie passed the folder to Molly. "It's just a few forms you need to complete."

Had Annie already mentioned Grace to Derek? No. Wasn't there some confidentiality rule or something? "Great. Thanks so much for bringing them over."

Molly accepted the papers. Her skin pebbled with goose bumps. Was she one step closer to welcoming Grace into her home? She glanced at Derek, who had his eye on the file. "Thank you so much. Let me walk you out."

"It was great to see you again, Derek." Annie shouted over her shoulder as she was rushed to the door.

"Same here, Annie. See you around." Derek waved.

Safe on the sidewalk, Molly clenched Annie's arm. "You didn't say anything to him, did you?"

"About Grace? No, of course not. Her information is confidential. But if I'm going to bring Grace by tomorrow to help with the painting, you might want to mention it to Derek."

"I know. I will." Annie gave Molly a quick hug before she scurried to her car parked along the curb. Apart from Annie, only Auntie Elsie knew about her dream of having a family. The last person she wanted to share the news with was Derek, but Grace's presence tomorrow would certainly raise some questions. It was best to tell him this evening.

Derek had never considered himself to be a nosy person, but he had to admit he was curious to know what was in the file. The moment Annie had passed it to Molly, it was as if something inside Molly shifted. He couldn't quite describe it. A combination of giddiness and joy, along with nervousness. After Annie left, Molly continued to snatch looks at the folder on the countertop. She kept a close eye on it and an even closer watch on him. Whenever he moved toward the mysterious package, her gaze followed.

"These extended roller brushes make painting so much easier," Molly called out over her shoulder.

"I thought it might help." Earlier, Derek had popped over to his store and brought the rest of the tools he had purchased for their project. Molly had made progress on the larger wall at the front. She looked adorable dressed in bib overalls, with dots of paint spattered on her cheeks and her hair pulled back in a ponytail. He struggled to keep his focus on the job.

"Watch—"

Splat.

Before Derek had time to react to Molly's warning, he'd stepped into the shallow plastic tray of paint. His ankles were splattered in blue.

Giggling, Molly climbed off the stepladder. "Hold on a minute. I'll get some paper towels from the restroom." She headed to the back of the store.

"Thanks." He glanced down at the tray. Thankfully, not much paint had gone to waste.

"Here you go." Molly offered him a handful of towels. "You didn't hurt yourself, did you?"

If he hadn't had his eyes glued on Molly, this wouldn't have happened.

"Nah. I'm fine." He reached for the paper towels, and his fingertips brushed hers. A tingling sensation shot up his arm. What was going on? It was like he was on one of those carnival rides where the floor dropped out from under you. He'd loved those as a kid. Today, it wasn't as fun. Did she feel it, too? Her look said maybe so. This wasn't good. "Thanks. I'll clean it."

A knock at the front door sent a wave of relief through him. "That must be Greg." Good. He needed Greg as a buffer. Something was happening here. But he couldn't allow any romantic feelings to take root. Love led to marriage, and he knew how that story ended. Painfully. For everyone involved. His goal was twofold. He needed to fulfill his promise to Rusty to help Molly, and also focus on buying the two spaces. That was the plan. Nothing more.

Two hours later, the store buzzed with activity. Greg's hammering and drilling drowned out the music Molly had turned on earlier. The bookcases were coming along. Greg was a pro. At this rate, he'd finish up tonight.

"I think it might be time to take a break." Molly yanked on the tarp protecting the floor and slid it further down the baseboard. "If you'd like, I can call in a pizza for dinner."

Food. Exactly what he needed to get his focus off Molly. "Pizza sounds great." Derek headed toward Greg. "What do you say? Are you hungry, Greg?"

"Oh no, man. Lila is roasting a chicken tonight. I told her I'd be home in time for dinner. Thanks for the offer though."

Dinner alone with Molly? This wasn't what he had planned.

Molly made her way across the room. "I'm sorry you can't join us, Greg."

"Yeah, thanks, Molly, but I'm going to finish up the job here and then head home to my family." Greg turned his focus back to the task at hand.

"Do you still love mushrooms on your pizza?" Derek's question broke the silence hanging in the air. Practically every Saturday night, the gang had gone to Mikos for pizza night. It was popular with the college crowd. Of course, Molly had always sat side by side with Ryan.

Molly glanced over her shoulder. "How did you remember I love mushrooms on my pie?"

Derek wrinkled his nose. "Because I can't stand them. I'm an extra cheese and onion guy." He remembered a lot of things about Molly. She was the kind of person who left an impression.

"Fair enough." Molly pivoted on her heel and headed toward the store's landline behind the counter. "So one large with half mushroom and half extra cheese with onion?"

Derek slipped his wallet from his back pocket and pulled out his credit card. He approached Molly and offered the plastic. "Here, it's my treat."

"I want to pay as a thank-you for your help." Her gaze slid toward the ground.

The gesture was nice, except she couldn't afford it. But he didn't want to make her feel bad by denying her offer. "This is on Rusty. He owes us for our manual labor." He winked, and Molly accepted the card.

Later, as Molly continued to paint some of the baseboard along the front of the store, Derek greeted the teenage delivery driver at the front door. The aroma of onions infused his nose, and his stomach grumbled in response. "Mmm…it smells good." He ran the box underneath his chin and placed the pizza along with the beverages on a nearby table. Derek removed his leather wallet from his back pocket. "Thanks a lot." He passed a ten-dollar bill to the boy.

"Wow! Thank you. I've never gotten a tip this big." His eyes widened.

"I used to deliver pizza myself when I was your age."

Derek smiled and waved goodbye. He recalled the first five-dollar bill he'd received when he made deliveries as a young boy. His father had put it in a frame and praised him. *I'm proud of you, son. A good work ethic is as important as your word. Don't forget that.* His word. Yeah, right. He also said family was important. If that were true, why had he destroyed theirs? Forcing thoughts of his father from his mind, he took the food and headed toward the counter.

"It was nice of you to give the boy such a generous tip," Molly remarked.

"Have you seen the price of a movie these days? The poor kid will have to deliver a lot of pizzas if he wants to go out on a date." Derek placed the food on the counter and reached for the file Annie had dropped off earlier.

"Don't touch that!" Molly's tone was sharp as a razor, and her face was a fiery red. With lightning speed, she snatched the folder from Derek's hands.

"I'm sorry. I wanted to move it out of the way so we could eat. I didn't want to spill anything on it." Earlier, Annie had mentioned to Derek she worked as a social worker, but she'd remained quiet as to the contents of the file. It couldn't have anything to do with the bookstore. A social worker wouldn't get involved in a failing business. As Derek watched, Molly scurried back to her office with the file held as if it were a newborn baby. Why was she reluctant to talk about it? Like his father, did Molly have secrets?

Chapter Six

The following morning, before sunrise, Molly pushed the key into the lock of her store and turned the knob. Inside, the smell of yesterday's painting project lingered in the air. Molly flipped the light switch and giggled when she spotted the tarp with Derek's footprint.

She knew she'd overreacted last night when Derek moved the file that Annie had dropped off. Her nerves were rattled by the idea of sharing her dream with Derek. Getting married had been one of her dreams, and look what he'd done to that. In the end, she didn't mention her adoption plan. This morning, she had no choice. Annie would be bringing Grace to the shop in a couple of hours. She needed a plan, but first, she needed coffee. A glance at her watch told her Derek's shop wouldn't be open for another hour.

Molly moved toward the counter to stow her purse. Her gaze passed over a piece of paper positioned next to last night's empty pizza box. *Mols, I'll be back in a few with coffee. I know you need it. D.* The small smiley face at the end of his note sparked a smile to part Molly's lips. It quickly slipped away. Wait. How did he get in here? She scanned the room. The wall left half-painted last night when they'd quit for the evening had been completed. Did the man ever sleep?

"Good morning." The deep voice filled the store. "Is it okay if Duke joins us?"

Molly whirled around, and her breath hitched at the sight of Derek standing at the entrance dressed in jeans, a sweatshirt and a baseball cap turned backwards. He looked like the college boy from years past. In his hands were two large coffee cups and a brown bag. At his feet was the puppy she'd seen the first day he returned to Whispering Slopes. The animal's tail moved like windshield wipers in a downpour. The puppy let out a yelp as though asking permission to enter.

How could she refuse? Molly smiled. As a little girl, she'd always wanted a puppy of her own. But moving from home to home, she'd learned not to get attached to any pet or their owners. "Of course Duke is welcome."

Derek bent down and released the leash from the dog's leather collar.

Molly knelt, and the puppy's toenails scuffed across the floor as he raced toward her, his body not yet catching up with his oversized paws. He skidded to a stop, and Molly scooped the animal into her arms. "Aren't you the cutest thing." She giggled as Duke covered her cheek with his tongue.

Derek glided around the room and approached the counter. "I think he likes you." He reached inside his pocket and removed a dog treat. "Come on, Duke, you big flirt, we've got work to do."

Molly placed Duke back on the ground so he could investigate the snack.

"Did you get my note?" Derek asked as he moved closer.

The scent of pine trees after an early snow tickled her nose. "I did."

Derek offered one of the cups. He placed the bag on the counter and began to dig inside. First, he removed two napkins and spread one out in front of where she stood. He reached back inside the bag with an extra napkin and held her gaze. "You're going to love this."

Molly watched as he slowly removed a large, glistening glazed doughnut. Her second favorite.

"Try this." He passed the decadent morning treat to her.

Sinking her teeth into the sugary pillow, she closed her eyes for a second. "Ah…it's still warm."

Derek nodded. "That's when they're the best." He plunged his hand inside the bag again, this time forgoing the napkin. He pulled out his portion and took a massive bite.

Molly laughed and quickly covered her mouth. "I think you could finish it in two bites."

He flashed a sheepish grin and took another oversized bite. He chewed and swallowed the treat. "I think you're right. Remember the doughnut shop we used to hit during exam week? What was the name of that place?"

How could she forget? It was the reason she'd gained the dreaded freshman fifteen. The fifteen pounds they said every college student gained their first semester away at school. It was also the first place Ryan had ever taken her to. After cramming for their art history exam, he'd suggested they were in need of sugar to keep them going. It had been the start of a relationship that lasted their four years in college.

Following graduation, they'd agreed to go their separate ways after he accepted a job overseas. Seven years later, both still single, they'd reunited at a mutual friend's wedding, and quickly gotten engaged. Even now, at the age of thirty-two, Molly still hadn't surrendered her love of doughnuts. She'd had a fondness for them long before she'd ever met Ryan. "The Doughnut Hole. To this day, I haven't found a place that makes a better German chocolate cake doughnut."

"I remember you loved them. I tried to order that flavor this morning, but they were already sold out."

Wait. First, he'd remembered she loved mushrooms, and now her favorite doughnuts?

"Well, thank you. That was thoughtful. Can I ask a question though?"

"Sure."

"How did you get inside my store?"

Derek raked his hand along his stubbled chin. "Oh yeah. I hope you don't mind, but last night, after we finished, I called Rusty and asked if I could stop by his place to grab a spare key so I could come back in and finish that wall. Don't worry, I'll return it when we're done."

Molly raised her left brow and took the last bite of her doughnut.

"And I promise not to make a copy." He winked before taking a swig of his coffee. "I knew I wouldn't sleep well last night, so I figured I would finish up the wall over there."

"I could have completed the work this morning." Molly folded her arms over her chest.

"I have no doubt you would, but I'm anxious to paint the children's section. I think it's going to be great."

Derek's steady and confident tone settled her weary nerves. "But will it be enough?" Would making all of these improvements have an impact on her bottom line? A year from now, would she still own this business? She ran her hand along the smooth surface of the counter. Would sweet Grace be a permanent part of her life?

"Of course, it will be great. But we have a lot more work to do. I guess that's the reason why I couldn't sleep and why I decided to come in early to paint. Time is of the essence. We need to move as quickly as possible. I was surfing the internet last night, and I scored some of those child-sized rocking chairs. I put eight on hold if you want to go take a look at them this afternoon. The sooner we can get them here, the faster we can paint them."

"Where do I need to go?"

Derek shook his head. "Not you—us. We're going to take a road trip to Lexington later today. The caffeine is starting to kick in, so I can paint the bookcases."

"Starting to kick in?" Derek could run to

Lexington. "I can help with the painting, but I need to talk to you about something first." Her upper teeth dug into her lower lip.

"Is everything okay?"

"Yes, I just wanted to explain something." Her stomach twisted. "The file Annie dropped off yesterday, it pertains to an adoption."

Derek's brow crinkled.

"I plan to adopt a child—a little girl. Her name is Grace. Annie is going to drop her off this morning so I can spend some time with her."

"Wow…adoption. That's pretty life-changing."

She gulped a breath of air. Derek was right. If the adoption was successful, her life would never be the same again. But it was her dream. To have a family, someone she could love and who would love her in return. It's what she desperately wanted.

"Can you afford it?"

Molly bit down on her lip to keep her mouth from blurting out what was going through her mind. Who did he think he was to question what she did with her life? But in truth, she knew it was an intelligent question for him to ask. He was aware of her dire financial situation. It made perfect sense for him to question why she'd want to bring a child into the picture.

"Oh man. I'm sorry, Molly. My question was totally out of line. Please, accept my apology."

"No, you're right." She dropped her arms to her side. "I can't afford it, but when I started the adoption process, my business was doing well. It was before the big chain store moved in and demolished my dream of owning my own business." Her eyes brimmed with tears. She tried to hold back, but it was no use.

Derek stepped closer. "Please don't cry. We'll get your sales booming again. You'll be able to make a home for Grace. I promise."

Molly let his words sink in, but she wasn't sure if she could believe him. What if she couldn't bring her store back to life? If she was forced to close the shop, she'd lose her opportunity to adopt Grace. Her dream of having a child would be shattered, along with her heart.

Derek cleared the napkins, downed the last of his coffee and grabbed the empty bag. "Well, we better get started painting. I'm excited to meet Grace."

Was this guy for real? In less than twenty-four hours, he'd orchestrated the painting of her shop, along with the construction of new bookshelves, and he'd ordered chairs for her. His words appeared sincere, like he cared what happened to her business and with the adoption. But was it all an act? In the brief time he'd been in Whispering Slopes, his store was already successful. She'd seen the crowds coming and going. He didn't want to fail. Still, he appeared concerned about her well-being. Was it possible he wasn't the same man who sabotaged her wedding day?

At nine o'clock on the dot, the brass bell over the door sounded, announcing Grace's arrival. Duke sprang from the pillow Derek had placed in a nearby corner and sprinted toward the front of the store.

Molly placed her brush on the tarp. If she'd turned a second later, she wouldn't have seen Grace's face light up with joy as the child dropped to the ground to greet the rambunctious puppy. Like earlier with Molly, Duke smothered the child's face with wet kisses.

Derek turned to Molly. "Duke loves kids."

"Well, who do we have here?" Annie bent over and scratched the puppy's head.

"This is Duke." Derek squatted next to the child. "And you must be Grace. It's nice to meet you."

"Grace, this is Mr. Derek. He's a friend of Miss Molly's." Annie made the introductions.

"Hi," Grace chirped to Derek before turning her attention back to Duke. The dog licked the child's hand as though she had drips from an ice cream cone on her skin.

Annie gazed toward the children's section of the store. "I'm not so sure how much help Grace will be with the painting with Duke here."

"That's okay. It will be nice to have her around," Derek responded in a gentle tone.

Molly saw the warmth in Derek's eyes as he watched Grace play with Duke. Did Derek like children? Did he dream of having a family of his own like she did?

"Okay then." Annie tugged on her purse strap. "I'll be back at noon. Grace, I'll see you then, and we'll get some lunch."

The child remained oblivious to all of the adults in the room. Molly couldn't blame her. Grace probably didn't trust adults. Molly hadn't as a child. It would take time to break through those walls, but she would keep trying. The joy she felt in Grace's presence was something worth fighting for.

Three hours later, Derek sat behind the wheel of his Escalade SUV. When the light turned red, he snuck a peek at Molly. Her right knee bounced up and down. She looked as though she carried the weight of the world on her slender shoulders. "You okay over there?"

She nodded, but her body language told a different story. Earlier, he and Molly had finished up the painting while Grace had focused all of her attention on Duke. Now, fifteen minutes into their road trip to pick up the chairs, Duke was back at Derek's shop, and Grace was with Annie. Molly hadn't uttered a word since they left the bookstore. "Grace seems sweet."

Molly's eyes remained glued to the windshield. "I don't think Grace likes me." Her tone sounded defeated.

"What makes you say that?" Derek eased his foot off the gas pedal and took in the landscape filled with endless blue sky and treetops beginning to change color.

"This is my second visit with her, and we've barely talked to each other." Molly sighed. "I don't feel like we're connecting."

Having been raised in a small family with no siblings or cousins, Derek didn't know too much about kids. "Maybe she's just shy."

"I thought about that, but I get the sense she doesn't trust me. Given her experience so far in foster care, I'm not surprised. But I want her to know I'm not like the others."

As a child, Derek had always trusted adults—especially his father. Maybe he should have been more like Grace and kept his guard up and his expectations low. "You just need to give it time, Molly."

A brief silence lingered inside the car.

"Maybe so. I suppose I'm feeling a little sorry for myself." She pulled down the window visor as a ray of sun peeked over the mountainside. "I guess I'm just a little jealous of your dog."

Derek laughed. "Duke? Why?"

"Grace obviously fell in love with him. I couldn't tear her away from Duke to help us with the painting."

"I don't think that had anything to do with you. You shouldn't take her reaction to Duke personally. What kid wouldn't rather play with a puppy than do manual labor?"

"You're probably right." Molly didn't sound too convinced.

"Of course I am. You'll have a breakthrough with Grace. Just be patient."

A few miles up the road, Molly was still quiet. Derek had hoped the time together in the car would give him the opportunity to discover what she'd been doing the past two years, apart from running her store and pursuing adoption. Had she dated anyone since Ryan? Had she traveled anywhere exciting? But more importantly, would she ever be able to forgive him when she heard the entire story from him? Never one to beat around the bush, he needed answers. "So, do you ever hear from Ryan?"

"Are you serious?"

Oh boy. Bad timing. She couldn't walk away from the conversation. "Look, I know you might not want to talk about Ryan or your wedding day, but if we're going to continue to work together, it's something we need to discuss."

"I haven't talked to or seen Ryan since the day of the wedding." She ran her palms along the tops of her thighs. "He was your friend. Don't you hear from him?"

Derek simply shook his head.

"So there's no point in us talking about Ryan."

Derek's stomach knotted. This wasn't going as he'd planned, but he needed to make things right with their past. Ryan had been his best friend. They'd shared a childhood, along with many major events during their lives. First, they'd both had a crush on Lindy Jamieson in the first grade. In the end, they'd decided girls had cooties and their friendship meant more.

When Ryan told Derek he was in love with Molly and planned to propose, Derek had been the first to congratulate him. At the time, he'd been truly happy for his friend. He'd still believed in marriage and family. But that had all changed the morning of Molly and Ryan's wedding. The day he'd realized he didn't know his father. Didn't want to know him. A man who had broken his wedding vows. Still, his decision to tell Ryan marriages didn't last was wrong. Molly deserved to know the truth about that day, but now, with her arms crossed and her lips pursed, Derek knew this discussion was over…at least for the time being.

Chapter Seven

Molly and Derek stepped inside Anderson's Woodworks. She drew in a deep breath, and warm memories churned in her mind. In the summer following her sixth birthday, Walter and Angela Corbett had welcomed Molly into their custom-built ranch home.

Walter had owned and operated a sawmill on three hundred acres of rolling farmland in southern Virginia. Molly had spent hours with Walter watching the variety of woods as they were processed for furniture, flooring and staircases. She'd loved the aroma of freshly cut walnut, oak and maple trees. For the first time in her life, Molly had felt loved.

The couple had been unable to have children of their own. They'd been working with the local foster care system with hopes to adopt a child. Tragically, two weeks before the adoption process was to be finalized, the couple died in a car accident. Molly had never forgotten the sound of the school principal's high-heeled shoes tapping down the hallway as she escorted Molly from her classroom.

"So, do you think these will work?"

"What? I'm sorry, did you say something?" She needed to get a grip. Derek was trying to help her, but so far, this outing had done nothing but stoke memories, most of which she'd rather forget.

Derek took one of the small oak rocking chairs. "These are the ones I saw online. I reserved eight of them. We can purchase them today if you'd like. Or we can keep looking." He scanned the aisles of furniture.

Molly ran her hand along the smooth wood. She'd started a tally of all of the expenses mounting to pay for this makeover. She hoped her financial situation would improve like Derek promised, and she'd be in a position to reimburse him and Rusty. "These are perfect. Thank you for taking the time to do some research. I appreciate it." Her rude behavior earlier in the car ignited a wave of guilt. She hadn't been ready to talk with Derek about Ryan and what she'd overheard that day. Would she ever be?

After a moment of silence, he gazed in her

direction. "You're welcome." His eyes skimmed the wooden floor. "I'm sorry about the ride over here. I shouldn't have mentioned Ryan. Since we're working together, I thought it might be good to talk about what happened, but I was wrong."

In truth, it made perfect sense to discuss what he'd said to Ryan the day of the wedding and try to clear the air, but her heart wasn't cooperating. After two years, the pain festered like a wound unable to heal. He'd ruined her chance to fulfill her dream of becoming a wife and a mother. How could she ever trust another man after what Ryan had done? Derek had set the wheels in motion that day when he talked to Ryan, and now that he was here in Whispering Slopes, his presence had torn off the scab. Molly's throat seized. "Let's get those chairs."

Forty minutes later, the back of Derek's SUV was packed. "It's a good thing I didn't want more chairs." Molly scanned the furniture arranged like a jigsaw puzzle in order to utilize the most space.

"We can always make another trip if you decide you'd like to add a few more."

"I think this should be enough, but thanks." Molly couldn't deny Derek was making an effort. Was it time for her to meet him halfway and make the best of the situation? For better or worse, she needed his help if she were to have any chance at keeping her store open. Plus, he'd been generous with his time. "You must be starving. I know you think I'm destitute, but how about we stop for lunch? My treat."

Derek laughed. "Sounds great to me. Any suggestions?"

"I know just the place. It's about two miles down the road." Feeling a bit more relaxed, Molly settled back against the leather seat for the remainder of the ride.

"There it is. Turn right at the next entrance." She pointed to the sign off the side of the road.

"Bert's Redhots? I took you for more of a steak and lobster gal." Derek navigated the vehicle into the last open parking space. "This place must be good. It's packed."

"Bert serves the best dogs in the valley. You'll love it." Molly smiled and unfastened her seat belt. "Plus, the views are incredible, and they don't cost a thing." The couple headed toward the line that snaked around the food truck to place their order.

When they were settled at a wooden picnic table, Derek's eyes bulged. "Boy, you weren't kidding. This is the best." He sank his teeth into the potato roll bun for the second time. A gob of chili sauce flopped onto the paper plate, next to a mound of onion rings.

Molly laughed as she pointed to her chin. "Right there." She passed him a napkin to wipe away the sauce.

"Thanks. These are messy, but so worth it."

"Around four years ago, Bert used most of his savings to buy and refurbish the old truck. Once he parked it here and word got out, people from all over the valley traveled for miles. Can you blame them?" She pointed to the surrounding mountains with hints of red and yellow ready to explode in splendid autumn color.

"He couldn't have picked a better spot." He plucked a crispy onion off his plate and popped it into his mouth.

Molly dabbed the napkin to her lips and took in her surroundings. "I've always loved the view here. Building a home on this road would be a dream come true. Could you imagine stepping out onto your back porch with a cup of coffee and seeing that view?"

Derek fingered the edge of his plate. "It sure is prime real estate. There seems to be a lot of available land."

"There is. I was raised down the road." Molly's mother had never been a homeowner. She'd rented a house and made it feel like her own.

"So your family owns land here?"

"No. My adoptive mother could never afford

to purchase a home for us. After she passed away, I moved closer to town."

"Rusty mentioned your mother. I'm sorry. How long has she been gone?"

Molly glanced toward the sky. She hadn't talked about her for a long time. Being close to the place her mother loved made it easier. "It's been two years." She watched as though she could see Derek calculating the timeline. When his eyes widened, she knew he'd realized.

"After your wedding day?" His face flushed.

"What was supposed to be my wedding day. Yes. She'd been undergoing treatment for breast cancer. A year after her diagnosis, the doctors discovered it had spread. She passed away three days after I was to be married."

The silence was broken by a male and a female cardinal singing in a nearby evergreen. With timid movements, Derek reached across the table and rested his hand on top of hers. Warmth conflicted with the chills traveling through her body.

"I'm so sorry you lost your mother. I also want to apologize for what happened at the church."

"Derek, I appreciate everything you've done for me. I do, but I'm not ready to talk about this with you." She paused. "I thought I was, but right now, I need to focus on my store."

All of these discussions about the past were causing the pain to bubble back to the surface. Compartmentalizing was her way to lighten the emotional baggage she'd accumulated since childhood. She wasn't ready to open her internal container and sort through its contents. Not now. And certainly not with Derek, of all people.

Later in the evening, Molly tried to settle her racing mind by baking homemade chocolate chip cookies. Gripping the side of the yellow mixing bowl, she stirred in two eggs, along with a teaspoon of vanilla. She mixed the ingredients, unable to escape the events from earlier in the day. Why had she mentioned her mother during lunch? Before, she'd been enjoying herself and his company.

Of course getting close to Derek wasn't a good idea. Yet there were moments when she felt drawn to him. *Stop, Molly. You need to keep your emotions in check. Otherwise you'll be hurt again.*

Using the cookie scoop, she formed the dough into perfect round balls. One by one, she spread them out onto the baking tray. The oven beeped, indicating it was preheated. Molly lifted the tray and noticed one of the balls wasn't shaped like the rest. Her mind drifted to the countless foster homes she'd lived in after Walter and Angela passed away. Molly had done everything she could to be the perfect child while in each home. She'd wanted the adults to fall in love with her and offer her the forever home she dreamed of having.

As she raised her hand to smash the dough and reshape it, she thought of Ryan. His parents hadn't thought she was good enough. He'd never said it, but it had been obvious by their actions. They'd wanted him to marry someone with similar breeding, not a woman raised in foster care. They were probably happy when their son left her at the altar after his conversation with Derek. She slid the tray into the oven, leaving that one piece of dough malformed. Like her.

You'll never be perfect enough.

An hour and a half later, with warm cookies sealed in a plastic container to take to the store tomorrow, the scent of sweet vanilla filled the house. Molly snuggled into an oversized chair in her bedroom. The cup of tea in her hands sent ribbons of steam trailing underneath her chin. She flipped through the file documenting Grace's life in foster care. Her stomach turned over as she read accounts of abuse. One home in particular revealed stories too horrific to read. *No!* Barely able to breathe, she tossed the file aside. *Lord, please, tell me what to do. Am I strong enough to do this?*

Silence engulfed the room before her attention was once again drawn to the file. A sense of calmness and strength replaced the fear. Molly reached for her phone resting on the table. As she tapped out a text, the weight against her chest continued to ease. When can I see Grace? She hit Send, and her message was on its way to Annie.

Derek's jaw tightened as he struggled to review the inventory on his laptop. He couldn't stop thinking about his conversation with Molly yesterday. The guilt had dug a little deeper when she'd mentioned her mother had passed away three days after he'd ruined her wedding day. Yesterday, he had wanted to tell her everything, but maybe she was right. Now their focus should be on saving her store.

Following a sleepless night, he'd headed to his coffee shop just before sunrise. The email he'd received from his mother late yesterday had also contributed to his inability to sleep. His eyes brimmed with tears. His father was ill, nothing serious, but she stressed it was time for Derek to forgive him. After a year of therapy and legal proceedings, Derek's mother had divorced his father. He'd asked for her forgiveness, and she'd given it to him. She was a Godly woman. Derek couldn't see himself following in her footsteps. How could he? His entire childhood had been one big ruse.

Three long hours later, and with the inventory now complete, Derek stepped out from his office and into the store. The place was a flurry of activity. With Charles and Nell in charge, he was comfortable leaving to help Molly work on the children's section. His store was certainly in capable hands.

"I'll be next door if you two need anything."

Charles shot him a glance from behind the counter. "We've got everything covered."

The long line flowing with ease was proof. "Thanks, guys. Remember, tomorrow we'll be giving out the discount to any customer who shows a receipt of ten dollars or more from Molly's store." Derek had used an online printing company to design coupons resembling a business card and had paid for expedited delivery.

"Will do, Boss. I'll get that sign up that we talked about," Charles answered.

"Do you want to take Molly some coffee?" Nell called out as she wiped down one of the bistro tables.

"That's a great idea."

Outside the store, with Molly's beverage in

hand, Derek was met with resistance when he pulled on the door handle. The lights were on, so he knew she was inside. He tapped on the glass so he wouldn't startle her.

Molly emerged from the back room. She breezed through the store dressed in faded blue jeans and a pink sweatshirt. Her hair was swept into a messy bun with loose tendrils framing her face. Derek's pulse accelerated.

She opened the door and gave him a half smile. "Good morning." Her eyes lasered in on the coffee.

He passed her the cup. "It's a new blend. I hope you like it."

"Thank you. I could use some caffeine this morning." So he wasn't the only one who couldn't sleep last night. She stepped to the side as he entered the store. He moved slowly, enjoying her fragrance.

Molly took a drink of her beverage before turning to Derek. "I baked some cookies last night. They're on the counter." She pointed. "Would you rather start work on the walls or the rocking chairs?"

"Thanks for the cookies." He rubbed his hand underneath his chin. "Well, since the excited bookworms are set to come to Book Buddies, we should start on the chairs so they'll be ready by Wednesday."

She nodded. "I was happy when the school called. This class hadn't been assigned a book to read in advance due to the short notice, but I'll pick something out. It's a class of first-grade students, so I'll read a book to them. I'd love to have the space ready for them to use, but I can't have the children sitting on wet paint."

Derek laughed as he palmed his face. "Yeah, you're right. We can work together on the chairs and take care of the walls afterward, so the rockers will have plenty of time to dry."

"Sounds like a plan."

"By the way, I reminded Charles and Nell that tomorrow we'll start distributing the coupons with proof of purchase from your store. Charles is going to make up a sign to put at the front of my store. Hopefully, this will send people to your shop before they come in for their coffee purchase."

Molly unrolled the tarp she'd brought from the storage closet earlier. The buckets of yellow and blue paint were lined up against the wall. "Thanks. I can use all of the help I can get."

Derek pulled the screwdriver from his back pocket and bent over to pry off the lid. "Last night, I came up with more ways to increase traffic."

"You've confirmed my theory."

He turned in her direction and placed the can at her feet. "What's that?"

"You must never sleep at night."

"Well, not much." In the past two years, he hadn't clocked much sleep. Between store openings and thinking about his father, sleepless nights had become the new normal.

"So, what's your idea?"

"Last night, I did an internet search for Bound to Please Reads. Guess what I found?"

"I don't know…what?"

Derek couldn't believe it. "Do you mean to tell me you've never done a search on your store?"

"Why would I do that?"

"Come on, Molly. Next you're going to tell me you still use the telephone book." Derek laughed. "If you ever hope to compete with the large chain stores, you need to have a presence in cyberspace. Everyone is online these days—especially businesses."

"I guess you're right."

"There's no guessing involved. I'm serious. You need a website and a newsletter."

"What in the world would I write about in a newsletter? How my sales are so low? Oh, I know. Why don't I write about the going-out-of-business sale I'll be forced to have if things don't improve in the next couple of weeks? Or how about how I could lose my house?"

It was obvious she was taking this the wrong way. "I'm not trying to be critical. Let me give you an example. Say I live in Tennessee, and I'm planning a trip to Whispering Slopes. The first thing I'm going to do is search the internet for things to do and places to go. Think of all the out-of-town visitors you're missing. They're all going to your competitor to purchase the book they plan to read while on vacation."

Molly removed a paintbrush from a bucket of supplies. She dipped it in the can of yellow paint and wiped the excess on the rim. "I see your point, but I don't know a thing about creating a website or a newsletter." She moved toward one of the rockers and sat on the floor, pulling the paint can toward her. With one stroke, she brushed the seat and glanced in his direction. "And don't forget, it's not like I'm in a position to hire someone to do all of this."

It pained him to see Molly struggling. God had blessed him with a head for business that had provided him with financial security. He wanted to help her as much as he could. "Have you ever learned how to do something on You-Tube?" He opened the blue paint, grabbed a brush and joined Molly on the floor.

"The other day, I learned how to fix my leaky toilet."

Derek laughed. "See, you can find anything on the web."

"I know, it sounds silly. But a couple weeks ago, I did teach myself how to make the most delicious lasagna. It's incredible."

"I love lasagna." He rubbed his stomach. "I can show you a few excellent videos on how to create your website and a newsletter."

"I don't know. When it comes to technology, I've always been challenged."

"When I opened my first coffee shop, I didn't know anything about building a presence on the internet, and my computer skills were lacking."

"They were?"

"Honest. I'll help you…but it will cost you."

She swiped her brush into the paint and resumed the task at hand. "I'll have to wait until my circumstances improve before I invest any money in advertising."

"Lasagna." He felt a grin pull at his cheeks.

Molly looked over as Derek turned the rocker to paint the other side. "Excuse me?"

"You can pay me with the amazing lasagna you learned how to make."

Her face reddened. "You want me to cook for you?"

"I can help."

"With the website?" Her brow arched.

"No. Well, yeah, with the website. But I can help you with the cooking, too." His suggestion surprised him as much as it had probably shocked her. She did a double take as though he had three heads.

"You want to cook together?"

"Think of it more as a working dinner. We'll get your website up and can celebrate with a nice meal."

Molly remained silent. He clung to hope. She could go either way. "I'll even do the dishes," he added.

Sweet laughter filled the room. "Okay, as long as you promise you'll help with the cleanup."

Derek crossed his heart. "You have my word."

"So, when do you want to do this?" Molly moved on to the next rocking chair.

"How about tonight?"

Molly's eyes popped open. "Seriously?"

"Yeah, the sooner we can get your website designed, the faster you'll start to bring in more customers. We need to get your business booming in order to keep your store open. I want you to welcome Grace into your home and give her the life she deserves."

The idea of spending more time with Molly caused his insides to vibrate like a rattlesnake's tail. Was that a good idea? Probably not. But Derek didn't care what his mind was telling him. For the first time in years, he was listening to his heart. And boy, was it speaking an entirely different language.

Chapter Eight

What in the world had she been thinking? She hadn't been. That was the only explanation. Monday evening, Molly pulled the container of whole milk ricotta cheese from the reusable canvas grocery bag. How had she ever allowed Derek McKinney to convince her to cook him dinner tonight? Oh right. They would be cooking together. Even worse!

The thought of working side by side at her kitchen island with Derek, slicing and dicing, turned her stomach into a knotted ball. She glanced at the wall clock, and her shoulders tensed. He'd be here in less than an hour, and she still needed to tidy things and grab a shower. She removed two cans of tomato paste, folded the sack and stowed it inside the pantry before she headed to her bedroom to get ready for her guest.

Later, when the doorbell rang, Molly bit the inside of her mouth. Dressed in her skinny black jeans and a lime-green cardigan, she fluffed the back of her hair cascading loose over her shoulders. *Here we go*. Releasing a deep breath, she hurried down the hall to greet her company.

"Good evening." Derek stepped inside holding a cluster of flowers.

Unsteady, Molly grabbed the edge of the door. He wore a smile that could melt a stick of butter long forgotten in the back of the freezer.

It was the flowers making her feel wobbly. Wasn't it? "Zinnias. I've always loved them." Wait. Was this another thing he remembered about her? They'd always been her favorite.

"I know." He handed her the flowers. "I remember seeing them in a beveled glass vase on your desk the few times I came to your dorm room with Ryan."

The vase. Molly's mother had given it to her when she graduated from high school. It had belonged to her mother, Molly's grandmother. How on earth had he remembered the only heirloom that meant the world to her? "Thank you. They are beautiful. Let me put these in some water, and we can get to work."

Derek looked around. "I brought my laptop. Where would you like to set up?"

Molly eyed the black leather bag strapped over Derek's broad shoulder. "We can work in the kitchen. Follow me."

Several videos later, and after a great deal of time and effort on Derek's part while she watched, Bound to Please Reads had a presence out in cyberspace. He'd registered her domain name as he explained webhosting and search engines along with other technological terms she'd never heard of. In addition, he'd set up several social media accounts.

"The website looks great, Derek. I could never have done this without your help. Thank you so much." She meant it. This would have taken her days or even weeks. Who was she kidding? She'd never have been able to figure it out.

"You're welcome. I enjoy this. It's fun for me. If you'd like, we can play around with your branding and add the newsletter sign-up after we get dinner started."

"Yeah, the newsletter. I thought about it after you mentioned it earlier. How often would you recommend I send one?" She had a hard time imagining who would read such a thing.

"I can tell you're not quite on board with this whole letter thing, are you?"

Over the years, Molly had signed up for hundreds of newsletters, but most went to her junk folder and were deleted. Who had the time to read them?

"I can't help but wonder, if I invest the time and send one out a month, would anyone bother to read it?"

"Email marketing has been proven to be the most powerful tool a business owner can use. Trust me. You just have to give the recipient a good reason to open up the email. I'll show you later. I'm getting hungry." Derek closed his laptop and pushed away from the table. "You've got your website, so it's your turn to teach me how to make that amazing lasagna you raved about." He extended his hand to help her from the chair.

Molly flinched at the tingling sensation when their skin touched. Why did he have to be so charming? *You'd better keep far away from this man while cooking.* Whatever this feeling was, she couldn't get it again. She'd have to do her best to stay on her side of the granite countertop island. Her store and Grace were most important.

"Oh, I see this is the healthy lasagna." He nudged his shoulder against hers.

Molly moved away and placed the large cast iron skillet on the stove top. "What do you mean?"

"You've got ground beef and ground sausage

here." He pointed to the two meats Molly had laid out to defrost.

"I never mentioned the word *healthy*. But trust me, once you try it, you'll realize it's worth logging a few extra miles on the tread-mill." After placing the meat into the pan, she pulled an oversized spoon from the uten-sil drawer and began to separate the beef into small pieces. She repeated with the sausage.

Derek stood watching. "I thought we were going to do this together. I need an assign-ment."

Molly laughed. "You're right." She placed the spoon on the ceramic holder, opened the drawer again and pulled out a knife. Then she grabbed the large white onion from the coun-ter and passed both to Derek. "Here, you can dice this onion on the cutting board over there. While you're at it, go ahead and mince those five garlic cloves. Watch your fingers."

Derek reached for the board, moving it and himself closer toward her. His brow crinkled. "Okay, you got me."

"What do you mean?"

"Mince and dice. Isn't it the same thing? Chopping."

"You are a novice in the kitchen." She re-duced the heat under the skillet. "First, this is an onion. It's a vegetable."

"What? It's not a fruit?" Derek rolled his eyes. "So you want me to dice it. Like this?"

Molly shook her head. Without thinking, she reached for his hand. "That's too big. It should be cut into smaller, equal-sized cubes. Dicing should be half the size of chopped chunks." With their close proximity, his warm breath tickled the side of her neck. He smelled like a wintergreen mint. What happened to keeping him out of her personal space?

"This is more confusing than my geometry class in high school." He turned, and their eyes met for a split second before he looked back to his assigned task.

Once the onion was diced, Molly reached for the clove. "This is garlic. It's a close relative to the onion you chopped."

"Wait. Didn't I dice it? This is way too confusing."

"Funny. Next, you'll want to mince this guy." Once again, she placed her hand over his. "I think you can handle this. It's the easiest. Chop it as fine as you can, almost into a paste." She inched away from him and turned her attention back to the meat. Why was she breaking her own rules? *You could have told him how to do it. No more touching.* Molly steadied herself against the stove. She felt light-headed, and it wasn't due to hunger.

Less than two hours after their cooking lesson, Molly placed the overloaded plate in front of Derek.

"Wow! Is this for us to share?" His eyes widened at the large slice of lasagna oozing with cheese. "I shouldn't have eaten your delicious side salad first. It's filling critical space."

She'd neglected to tell him the recipe had called for a pound of mozzarella cheese and a cup of grated Parmesan cheese. She'd slipped it in while he was opening the cans of tomato paste. "Nope. It's all yours. The garlic bread is ready, too." Molly grabbed the potholder and strolled toward the oven.

"Oh man. You should have told me to wear my workout pants. They're elastic. I'm not sure the button on these jeans will hold."

"Well, make sure you leave room for dessert. I bought a chocolate cheesecake at the grocery store." She ferried the garlic bread to the table.

"It's a good thing we're not married. I wouldn't be able to fit in any of my clothes." He plunged his fork into the pasta.

His words stung. Married? To him? No way. Molly settled into her chair. It was best to let his comment go. "So, how does it taste?"

"You were right. I've never tasted lasagna as good as this in my life. You should forget the bookstore and open a restaurant." He dug in for another bite. "This stuff is amazing."

"I could never forget my store." She poked her fork at the cheese.

"I know you couldn't. I'm sorry."

Lately, Molly was questioning everything, including whether she was capable of running a business. But she couldn't give up. "I know you were joking." She glanced at his plate and was surprised to see half of his lasagna gone. "I'm glad you like it, because we'll have plenty left over for you to take home."

"Maybe not. I'm ready for another piece." His chair scraped across the hardwood as he stood. "Stay put. I can help myself."

Molly considered Derek's comment. It would be nice to one day cook a special meal for her husband. But Ryan, with Derek's help, had filled her head and heart with so much doubt when it came to relationships. She couldn't picture herself ever walking down the aisle again.

Following a major cleanup in the kitchen, Derek retrieved his laptop while Molly grabbed them each a bottle of water from the refrigerator. "Thanks again for helping with the dishes. It goes a lot faster with two people tackling the job." Was marriage like this? Working as a team, not only with big issues, but the everyday tasks? Earlier, Molly had found comfort standing side by side with Derek. Joking around while he rinsed the dishes and passed them along to her to load into the dishwasher was nice. She forced the thoughts away. She wouldn't allow herself to get close to Derek or any man.

Derek placed his computer on the kitchen table. "No problem. It's the least I can do after such a fantastic meal. I never knew you were such a great cook. It makes me wonder what other secrets you're keeping."

"Being a private person doesn't have to mean you're secretive." She passed the bottle of water to him.

He shrugged and unscrewed the cap. "I'm not so sure about that."

Molly opened her drink and took three sips before taking her seat at the table. "What do you mean?"

"Let's just say I have firsthand experience when it comes to secrets destroying lives." He powered up the laptop and tapped on the keys.

Did Derek think she'd kept secrets from Ryan? Had he convinced her fiancé there were things he didn't know about her? Why would he do something like that? She'd been honest with Ryan about her upbringing in foster care, but should she have told him about the abuse she'd endured?

During their relationship, she hadn't thought so, but now, speaking with Derek, she wasn't so sure. How could you enter into a marriage without being one hundred percent straightforward about the past? Those past experiences shaped who she was today. As she considered Derek's comment, it became obvious to Molly that he had some secrets of his own.

After Derek had made his proclamation about secrets, he kept quiet and worked on Molly's newsletter. He wasn't sure why he'd made the statement about secrets, but it was too late to take it back now. It was out there. Most likely, Molly had all sorts of questions. Thankfully, she remained silent and took notes as he went over how to design her email campaigns for the newsletter.

"Okay, I have your template ready. All you'll need to do is fill in the content each time you'd like to make an announcement."

"What would you suggest I include in my first letter?"

As she leaned in closer, a coconut aroma reminded him of family trips to the beach when he was a kid. Back when he'd believed he had a real family. He'd even dreamed of having his own one day. But thanks to his father's actions, he no longer had that dream. "You could announce your new website. It's all part of the goal to drive people to your webpage. Also, once we finish with upgrading the store, we can share some photographs. You could spotlight the children's area to promote your Wednesday night Book Buddies."

"Those are great ideas. But you'll help me with the first letter, right?"

Derek gazed at Molly. She pouted with her lower lip out like a child begging to stay awake past her bedtime.

"Of course I will."

Molly jumped at the sound of three loud knocks at the front door. "I wasn't expecting anyone."

Derek turned to the kitchen window. Nightfall had long settled in. "It's not a good idea to open your door after dark. I'll go with you."

"You're not in the big city." Moving toward the front of the house, Molly flipped on the dining room light located right off the foyer. A cherry table with four chairs filled the room. Derek noticed the jigsaw puzzle pieces spread across the top. Puzzling was one of his favorite things to do when he needed to settle his mind.

Once at the front door, Derek placed his arm in front of Molly. "Let me take a look." He turned on the porch light and spotted an elderly gray-haired woman pacing back and forth. "I think it's safe." He opened the door.

"Mrs. Whiteside. What are you doing out and about after dark?" Molly stepped outside.

"Jerry got loose. Have you seen him?"

"No, I'm sorry. I haven't. Do you want us to help you look for him?" Molly turned to Derek. "Jerry is Mrs. Whiteside's cat."

"We can grab a flashlight and look around if you'd like." Derek felt sorry for the woman. She reminded him of his grandmother. She also loved cats.

"Oh no. That's not necessary. It's close to his dinnertime, so he'll come back when he's hungry. Just let me know if he shows up here. I'm sorry to bother you two young people." The woman stepped off the porch. "Good night." Mrs. Whiteside stopped and turned. "The two of you make a nice couple." She smiled broadly and headed toward her home.

Derek was a little uncomfortable with the woman's comment. He had no intention of becoming a couple with Molly or anyone. His work was the only relationship he was interested in. He followed Molly back inside. "I sure hope she finds Jerry."

"He'll come home. This is pretty much a weekly occurrence." Molly laughed and closed the door.

"Hey, I noticed the puzzle over there." Derek pointed and moved in closer for a better look.

Molly followed. "Yeah, I used to work on them a lot when I was a little girl. Along with books, puzzles were my escape. I bought one last year when we had a big snowstorm forecast. I'd forgotten how much I enjoyed them. I always have one going on this table."

How sad to think Molly needed to escape from something as a child. Or was it someone? Derek pulled out a chair. "You're not going to believe this, but I use my dining room table for jigsaw puzzles, too. I could spend hours connecting the pieces. This one looks pretty tough, but I can see why you would want to work it. It's a beautiful photograph."

Molly slid into the chair next to Derek. "I love hummingbirds. When I saw this puzzle online, I had to order it."

Derek raised the box that was lying facedown. "Two thousand pieces? I'm impressed. I typically don't do more than one thousand."

"Like I said, I couldn't resist. During the summer months, I have at least four hummingbird feeders in my backyard garden."

The moment he placed the box down, Molly turned it facedown again. "I don't look at the photo while I'm working the puzzle."

"What? Don't you think that makes it more

difficult?" Derek was impressed. If he didn't study the box, he'd never finish.

Molly shrugged. "It's the way I do it." She chose a piece and found a connection. "Sometimes when I'm writing and get stuck in my story, puzzling helps me work through things. I think a lot about my characters while connecting the pieces."

"I feel the same. Not about writing, of course, but my business. I've brainstormed a lot of ideas while working a puzzle." When Derek bought his first house, his parents had purchased a gorgeous mahogany table as a housewarming gift. Growing up, his mother had always insisted they eat together as a family. Knowing her, buying the table was a subtle way to encourage him to settle down and start a family. That would never happen. Of course, he hadn't found a way to break the news to his mother. She'd always wanted grandchildren, and since Derek was an only child, she was counting on him to make that dream come true. He turned to Molly. "It's funny we don't use our tables for dining."

A quiet space hung between them.

Guilt gnawed at Derek. Molly shouldn't be using her dining room table for jigsaw puzzles. She should be sharing meals with a family of her own. A family she could've had by now if he hadn't brought her into the middle of his personal problems. He had to tell Molly what had transpired that day at the church between him and Ryan. But telling her now would push her further away from him and ruin his chance to help her turn her business around. And that could ruin her chance of welcoming Grace to her table permanently.

Chapter Nine

"Should I put the snickerdoodles on the counter, or would you like them in the children's area?" Early Wednesday afternoon, Caitlin hurried in through the front door of Bound to Please Reads carrying an oversized platter loaded with cookies.

"Oh my, those smell delicious." Molly's weakness for sweets always increased when she was anxious.

"I know, right? My car smells like buttery cinnamon. I couldn't keep my focus on the road."

"How much do I owe you?" Molly turned to get her wallet from the office.

Caitlin positioned herself at the counter. "Oh no. You don't have to pay me anything. I dropped by The Trout Run Bed-and-Breakfast. Meg said they were on the house." Caitlin placed the cookies down and took off her running jacket. "She wanted me to let you know that she'd hoped to bring the triplets by today, but she has some new guests checking in later this afternoon."

"How thoughtful of her." Molly's friend Meg Brennan, a trained physical therapist, had her hands full. Not only did she run the quaint bed-and-breakfast on her own, but her sister and brother-in-law had left town in the middle of the night and abandoned their three children. Triplets. Meg had taken them in and was raising them as her own. Molly opened her leather journal and scribbled a reminder to text Meg a thank-you and see if they could get together for lunch. "It might be best to take the cookies back to the children's area since some of the kids are too short to reach the counter."

"You got it. I'll move the jigsaw puzzle off the larger round table," Caitlin suggested. "By the way, I love the new paint. And this children's area looks fantastic. The tiny rocking chairs are adorable. What a great idea."

Molly stood from the high office chair behind the cash register and approached Caitlin. She had to agree. The remodeled area had been well worth the extra effort. "I can't take credit for the chairs. It was Derek's idea." Another one of his suggestions that had turned out to be a big hit. Since Molly had reopened the store, there had been a constant flow of customers purchasing books. Most of the business was thanks to the discount he was offering to anyone who brought in a receipt from her store. Another blessing of living in a small town... word travels fast.

The front bell sounded as two women entered the store.

"Welcome to Bound to Please Reads, ladies. Is there anything I can help you with today?" Molly moved toward the front of the store.

The younger of the two women turned and smiled. She was dressed in tan slacks and a cream-colored cardigan. "My mother and I are on our way to Washington, DC. We're looking for a travel guide. Is that something you stock?"

"We sure do. Follow me. We have a rather extensive travel and leisure section." Molly led the two ladies to the far corner of the store. "Is this your first visit to the DC area?"

This time, the older woman spoke. "When I was in high school, my senior class took a field trip to Washington." The lady chuckled. "Obviously, that was a long time ago. I know a lot has changed, so I wanted to visit once more and share the experience with my daughter. We live in Florida, and she's never traveled outside of the state."

"You're a long way from home. May I ask how you learned about my store?"

The older woman rested her hand on her daughter's arm. "Jenny is the techie in the family. She found you on the internet. Your website is beautiful."

If Molly was keeping score, Derek was winning by a landslide. Another one of his suggestions was a success. "That's nice of you to say. I'm pleased you liked the site."

Molly chewed her lower lip. Derek had mentioned his plans to make an announcement about the Book Buddies gathering on her website and on the Twitter account he'd created for her store. She hadn't expected it to generate so much interest, but since she'd arrived at the shop this morning, her phone had been ringing nonstop with questions from parents about the event. Some asked if a reservation was required. For real? People thought they'd need to reserve a space?

The phone behind the counter rang. "I'll get it." Caitlin scurried to answer. "Thank you for calling Bound to Please Reads. This is Caitlin. How may I help you? Sure, she's right here." Caitlin handed the phone over. "It's Annie."

The coffee Molly had earlier that morning churned deep in her stomach. What if Grace didn't have fun painting? Or worse, maybe the child had told Annie she didn't like Molly, but Grace had spent most of the time playing with Duke. "Hey, Annie. What's up?"

"I want to bring Grace over today for Book Buddies."

Molly picked at a loose thread on her blouse, and her heart lifted. "Sure. Of course."

"Don't worry. I'll respect your privacy. We'll pop in and hang out for a while so Grace can observe your interaction with other children. It might help her get to know you better, so she'll feel more at ease around you."

"Did she say something? Did she not enjoy herself on Sunday?" Molly rubbed her earlobe. After Annie and Grace left, she'd replayed her time spent with Grace over in her mind. She couldn't recall anything that would've caused Grace to be uneasy in her presence.

"Oh no. Of course not. She did mention Derek's puppy. She's just shy around people, that's all. Give her time and you'll gain her trust."

Given Grace's background, that was understandable. As a child, Molly had been distrustful of people. In many ways, that hadn't changed, especially when it came to men. "So, what time do you plan to stop by?"

"We should be there before five o'clock." Annie paused. "And, Molly, try and relax. Just be yourself. Grace will come around."

Molly disconnected the call and wrapped her arms tightly around her waist. She hoped Annie was right. What if Grace never felt a connection with her? She needed to brush away the negative thoughts and stay positive, like Derek. Hopefully, in a couple of hours, the bookstore would be packed with customers interested in buying books.

Later in the day, as dusk crept over the mountains, Molly glanced at the time on her phone. Chills traveled through her body. With a half hour until the start of Book Buddies, the store was more crowded than she'd ever seen it. As much as it pained her to admit, Derek was right. Everything he'd said about building a platform had been spot-on. Sending a newsletter on a regular basis might spark more business. She could ask Derek to help her with more ideas this evening. If he wasn't busy.

Children's giggles filled the shop, and Molly's heart soared. She loved to see a sense of excitement in young readers. Her mind drifted to Grace. Did she read books to escape real life? Had any adult in her young life introduced her to the joy of reading? If not, maybe Molly could.

The front doorbell tinkled. Molly turned and spotted Derek entering the shop. Dressed in a dark brown leather jacket and faded jeans, she had to admit he looked handsome. He approached, and a wide smile parted his lips. "It looks like you've got yourself plenty of buddies today."

Molly laughed and nodded. "I have to give you credit. Your ideas were brilliant. I've never had this many children attend. I haven't checked my website today, but by the looks of this crowd, you must have posted everything we discussed."

"I did." Derek nodded. "I also added an extra incentive for the parents."

"And what might that be?" Molly was impressed.

He fished in his back pocket. "Coupons for a free coffee. If you don't mind, I thought I could pass these out to the adults."

"What's to mind? Of course you can. Thank you so much." Molly watched Derek while he worked his way around the store, handing out his gifts. She couldn't help but notice the number of double takes many of the female customers did when he passed by. Why wouldn't they? He was easy on the eyes. But not hers.

"That sure was nice of Mr. McKinney," Caitlin said as she leaned in close while Molly continued to observe Derek work the room, commanding the attention of every woman he spoke with. Many giggled and blushed. Shaking her head, she pushed aside a twinge of jealousy. Oh brother. She didn't have time for this nonsense. She had a business to save.

Without warning, Molly's heart stopped. Grace. She was here. She clung tightly to Annie. Her honey-blond hair bounced off her shoulders each time she turned her head to take in her surroundings. The child paused when their eyes connected. Molly's pulse quickened. Was that a glimmer of a smile? Whatever it was, it faded, along with Molly's confidence.

Excited children and adults filled the store, and she lost sight of Grace. A group of parents worked their way toward the beverage table Molly and Caitlin had arranged near the fiction section. Molly searched the crowd. Her heart squeezed when she spotted Grace again. Derek was kneeling in front of her, showing her something on his phone. When the most beautiful smile Molly had ever seen ignited across the child's face, it stole her breath. Grace's tiny lips moved, but Molly couldn't hear her over the buzz of the crowd. She heard Derek's laughter while the two looked closer at his device. For a minute, she was jealous. Why hadn't Grace smiled and laughed when they were together?

An hour and a half later, Book Buddies had completed its most successful gathering in its nearly two-year history. The first-grade class appeared to have loved her book choice, a sweet tale of a kitten, her outdoor adventures and the friends she met along the way. The children shared their favorite parts of the story. Many loved the birds and butterflies, while others loved the hummingbirds and turtles. Unfortunately, Grace never uttered a peep, but she appeared to listen to the discussion. That was something—right? But Molly was saddened by her lack of engagement with the group.

At the register, Caitlin handled purchases while some of the adults rallied their children to head home. Countless parents thanked Molly for a wonderful evening and expressed their excitement for next week. She should have been elated by the great turnout, but Molly had once again failed to make any connection with Grace. She busied herself by clearing away the empty cups.

"We had a nice time, Molly," Annie said as she approached with Grace, but the child kept her distance and her gaze glued on the floor.

Longing for a connection, Molly turned from the refreshment table and looked down at Grace. "Did you get some cookies and juice, Grace?"

She responded with a quick nod. That was it? That was all she got before the child took off toward Derek. Sadness bubbled up in her. This was supposed to be her time with Grace. Derek was ruining things again.

"She seems to have developed a fondness for Derek." Annie smiled.

Molly considered her friend's comment. She observed the interaction between the child and Derek and craved something similar. "Earlier, what was he showing her on his phone?"

"Oh, they were watching a video of his puppy. Before Book Buddies, we ran into Derek walking Duke. I've never seen Grace that excited. Derek was so sweet and patient, allowing her to pet the animal. Duke loved the attention. Derek videotaped the dog licking Grace on the cheek. Since I've known Grace, I've never seen her engage with anyone like she has with Derek."

Molly watched as a hidden dimple in Grace's cheek appeared while she gazed at Derek. The child appeared to cling to his every word.

Molly wrapped her arms tightly around her chest. "Maybe I should get a dog or a kitten?"

Annie laughed. "I think you have enough on your plate. Oh, by the way, I suggested something to Derek and he was okay with the idea, but I wanted to run it by you."

"Sure."

Annie stole a quick glance toward Grace

before turning her attention back to Molly. "I hope you don't get mad. Believe me, I'm not trying to play matchmaker or anything."

Molly was confused. "Okay…but you've lost me. Are we talking about Grace or Derek?"

"Well…both. I think part of the reason Grace is comfortable with Derek is because of Duke. After church on Sunday, I thought it might be a good idea for us to take Grace on a picnic."

Molly's shoulders relaxed. "It sounds like the perfect outing for the three of us."

Annie half laughed. "Well, I meant the five of us. You, me, Grace, Derek and Duke."

She was joking. Wasn't she?

"I know you have mentioned your past issues with Derck, but I think he and Duke could help you and Grace bond. Please, let's give it a try. Just once. Doing this in a group may take some of the pressure off and allow you to be more yourself."

So far, the time she'd spent with Grace hadn't gone the way she had hoped. In fact, it had only filled her head with self-doubt. She questioned whether she'd be a good mother for Grace…or for any child. "Do you think a picnic is the answer?" Molly wondered how she could be more relaxed with Derek around.

Annie rested her hand on Molly's forearm. "I think it might be the way for you to connect with Grace. Don't worry so much. I know you'd like to see what's happening with Derek and Grace happen for you, too, but trust me, this is all good. Having Grace comfortable with your friends is a good thing." She adjusted her purse strap on her shoulder. "I need to grab Grace and get going. Derek is on board with the idea, so we'll talk tomorrow."

Friends? Derek wasn't a friend. He was a business acquaintance who was helping her out. Wait—Annie had already spoken with Derek? Her head spun.

A picnic might be a good idea. But why did it have to be with Derek? He wasn't in her close circle of friends. In fact, he was the one person she'd rather keep in her past. True, he was helping her with the store, but once sales increased, she planned to stay as far away from him as possible. How could having Grace get attached to him be a good thing? She'd have to think about that later. She moved toward the counter to assist Caitlin with the last couple of customers.

"Thanks for coming tonight. We hope you'll come back again," Caitlin said as she passed the bag of books to a mother and daughter.

"Good night," Molly added with a smile.

"Phew! What a night. I don't think I've ever been so busy." Caitlin tipped her head, and a brunette strand escaped her loose ponytail at the base of her neck.

"That's a good thing."

Molly spun around at the sound of Derek's voice. His presence unnerved her tonight.

"I think this might be your best sales day ever. Or at least the biggest I've worked." Caitlin reached for her bottle of water next to the cash register and took a long pull. "If it's okay, I'll get going. I've got to study for an exam in the morning."

"Sure. Thank you so much for all of your help, Caitlin."

"Anytime." Caitlin reached for her backpack stowed in a cabinet. "Good night, Mr. McKinney." The young girl glided across the floor and out of the front door.

Derek leaned against the counter and smiled. "Congratulations on a successful night. The kids and the parents obviously enjoyed themselves."

Mixed emotions swirled in Molly. She couldn't deny the large turnout tonight was due to Derek and his expert marketing skills. Extending an invitation through social media to parents of children outside of the school system had been a great idea. The man had a head for business. "I should be congratulating you. I saw what you posted on the website and on Twitter. It's the reason so many people attended. The moment I opened the shop this morning, the phone rang with people expressing interest. Some asked if they needed a reservation."

Derek slipped his hands into his back pockets. "I'm glad I could help."

"You went above and beyond. Thanks to you, I might be able to pay Rusty last month's rent."

"I'm happy for you." Derek spun on his heel and headed toward the entrance. He stopped short of the front door and turned. His expression appeared despondent. "Good night, Molly."

Why the subdued attitude? She'd expected him to be excited and ready to put a rush on the newsletter. Whatever. It was all for the best. She'd take care of the letter herself. Despite all of the good he'd done for her store, she hadn't forgotten about the past. Derek telling Ryan he shouldn't marry her was indefensible. And what about him and Grace? Molly felt like she was competing with Derek for the child's attention. He'd ruined her wedding day, but she wouldn't allow him to come between her and Grace.

Early the following morning, a strong gust of wind rattled the shutters on Derek's one-story ranch home, rousting him out of bed. No point wallowing underneath the sheets anyway. He'd been wide awake for hours, flipping from his back to his stomach.

Derek swung his legs out of the bed and onto the cool pine floor. Duke sprang to his feet from the oversized pillow where he slept in the corner and raced to the edge of the nightstand.

"Hey, buddy. Did that wind wake you, too?" Derek scratched the puppy's head, and the gesture was returned with sloppy wet licks. "How about we get some coffee and go for a walk?"

Fifteen minutes later, the sun ascended over the mountains dominating the horizon. Shades of red and pink shimmered in the sky. Dawn. A fresh start. His favorite part of the day. Derek pulled in a deep breath as he and Duke walked the trampled path surrounding the ten-acre property. The strong winds from earlier had subsided, leaving behind crisp and cool air. Although Derek had signed a month-to-month lease, he had the option to purchase the house and land if he decided to stay in Whispering Slopes. But why would he? After his parents divorced, he'd vowed to never plant roots or settle down.

"It's just you and me, right, bud?" Duke was all he needed. The unconditional love from an animal would never disappoint. *How could you do that to us, Dad? Mom and I loved you. We put our trust in you.* He tried to push the thoughts from his mind. But like a slick oil spill in the blue waters of the Caribbean, his entire upbringing had been tainted with deception. His stomach soured. He dumped his remaining coffee onto the dewy grass. Derek bent down and unhooked the leash. Duke took off toward the split-rail fence, his wet nose to the ground.

Derek ran the events of last night through his mind. Molly had had a good turnout, and hopefully, it would generate a lot of sales. She should have been elated, yet her face had told a different story, like she was mad about something. She'd tossed scrutinizing glances while he'd shown Grace the video of her and Duke. Was she envious? He'd been confused by Annie's invitation to go on a picnic. But after she explained how Grace came out of her shell around him and Duke, he couldn't say no. She was a delightful little girl. As much as he didn't want to admit it, she'd gotten into his heart. That couldn't be a good thing, could it? It was the reason he'd made such an abrupt exit last night after Book Buddies. He couldn't get attached to the child. Or to Molly. He'd only get hurt.

"Come on, Duke," Derek called out over the cooing mourning dove. "I've got a town full of people who need their caffeine fix."

Later, after some time spent with his Bible,

Derek was showered, shaved and behind the wheel of his SUV. Bright rays of sun prompted him to pull down the car's visor, but it didn't obstruct his view of the golden-yellow leaves dotted with orange painting the skyline. It was a perfect day to be outside.

His mind drifted. *A picnic.* What about Molly's plan to keep things business only? Had it been wise to agree to spend an afternoon with Molly and Grace? Something about Grace had prevented him from saying no to Annie's invitation. The child came to life around Duke.

Derek was familiar with animals being used in nursing homes as a form of therapy to combat loneliness. He'd seen it at the home where his grandmother lived before she went to be with the Lord. She'd told him the weekly interactions with the visiting dogs were the highlight of her day, since she didn't have much to look forward to. The unconditional love the animals showed the residents had kept his grandmother going. It was what had prompted him to say yes to Annie.

Upon entering the downtown city limits, he eased his foot off the accelerator and took in his surroundings. A sense of calmness washed over him. Whispering Slopes was a far cry from the hustle and bustle of cities where his other coffee shops were located. Since opening his store here, he couldn't remember the last time he'd felt more at peace. Well, he could, but he tried to avoid thinking about it. It was a period of time he referred to as "Before Destruction by Dad."

Derek's life had been divided into two pieces. The first was a picture-perfect childhood he'd made up in his young mind. A time filled with family vacations, sitting down to dinner each night, playing sports, watching old Western movies with a giant bowl of popcorn and spending time together at Christmas, even though his father had been rarely present. His mother had covered for her husband. She'd even convinced Derek that his father worked so hard because he loved his family. That had all come to an end. Ripped to shreds. Everything he'd once believed about family, love and the importance of keeping your word had been destroyed two years ago.

Arriving at his shop, he rounded the back of the building and navigated his SUV into an empty parking space. Placing the car in Park, he glanced to his left and spotted Molly's bright red VW Beetle. She was in early. He hoped she was calculating profits generated by her Book Buddies. For a second, he considered popping in to apologize for his abrupt departure yesterday, but he decided against it. How could he explain the reason he'd bolted was the way he felt whenever Grace was around? For the first time since learning about his father's indiscretions, Derek had imagined what it would be like to have a child of his own. He couldn't allow those thoughts to take root, so he'd left the store as soon as he said goodbye to Molly.

He climbed out of the vehicle and pushed the key fob to lock the door, which wasn't necessary in this town. One of the many things he loved about Whispering Slopes. As soon as Derek rounded the building and approached his store, Molly's door flew open. Her arms flailed and her red hair swung back and forth as she sprinted toward him. "Derek! You have to help me…my store is underwater!"

Chapter Ten

It wasn't a dream. She was wide awake. From the moment Molly had opened the store's front door and stepped inside, her shoes had squished in the standing water soaking the floor. Sounds of water running caused her stomach to flip-flop. This couldn't be happening.

"I need to turn off the water. Do you know where the main shutoff valve is located?" Derek shouted.

"I'm not sure. I called Rusty, but I got his voice mail. I left a message. I'll check the back for the shutoff."

Before Molly had a chance to blink an eye, Derek bolted toward the rear of the store. Water splashed from underneath his feet onto his jeans.

"The chairs!" Molly caught a glimpse of the freshly painted blue and yellow rocking chairs in the children's section, and her heart squeezed. Yesterday, the children attending Book Buddies had loved the newest addition to her store. She raced toward the rockers and grabbed two at a time. With lightning speed, she shot toward the checkout counter and placed the chairs on higher ground.

"I've got the water turned off." Derek entered the room and wiped his hands down the front of his jeans. "For future reference, the valve is in the utility room."

"Thank you." Molly sped to move the remaining rockers. "I don't want these to get damaged. The children loved them."

Derek followed her lead and headed across the floor. "It's going to be okay, Molly." He grabbed three chairs, drawing her attention to his biceps.

Once all of the seats were safe on higher ground, Molly placed her hands on her hips and released a heavy sigh. "Look at my store. It's ruined."

"It's not as bad as it looks. At least none of the books got wet. Rusty will get a water restoration company in here. They can have it dried out with their industrial fans in no time."

Time was something she didn't have. "I can't stay open with those huge fans blowing into customers' faces. If I'm forced to close for a couple of days, I'll never be able to pay Rusty or my creditors." *And what about Grace?*

Derek stepped in closer. "Try and stay calm. Let me try to call again. Once the pros take care of the water, we'll work around the fans. I've known a few book lovers in my life. Trust me, they won't let a breeze in their face keep them from buying a book. Plus, I've got the online purchase link on your website. Remember?"

Molly's shoulders relaxed. She'd forgotten. Just yesterday, Caitlin had shipped out a couple of orders generated through the website. "Yes, but—"

"But nothing. You're going to be reopened in no time." Derek glanced at his watch. "We've got a couple of hours before you even open. I didn't see a mop in your utility room, so let me run next door and grab mine."

Molly hardly realized when Derek left the shop. The water had been turned off, but the sound of a rushing river continued to roar in her head. *God, what are you trying to tell me? That I should close my shop since I don't have a chance against my competition? Should I forget about trying to adopt Grace?* This flood had to be a sign. Her shoulders stiffened. This place was her life. She couldn't go down without a fight. It wasn't what her mother had done.

She'd fought the cancer until the end. Oh, how she wished her mother was still alive.

"What in the world?"

Molly whirled around to the familiar voice. "Rusty. I left you a message."

"I got it. Joe and his crew from the water restoration company are on their way. What happened?" His question sounded like it was spoken in slow motion.

"I'm not sure. When I opened this morning, the water was gushing from a pipe in the storage closet. The floor was already underwater."

Rusty shot looks around the room. "Judging by the amount of water, it looks like it went on for quite a while."

She should have asked where the main shut-off valve was located when she first moved in. A business owner should know those things. But she didn't. "I'm sorry. I didn't know how to stop it. When I saw Derek pull in, I rushed to get him."

Rusty ran his hand across his nearly bald head. "This isn't good at all."

Molly could read his mind. If he'd accepted the investor's offer from the start, this wouldn't be his problem. But Rusty was a good man, and a dear friend to her mother. He'd made a promise to her mother that he'd look after her, and he was a man of his word.

The front door swung open for the second time in the past two minutes. Derek raced inside carrying a giant mop. It reminded her of the one Mr. Simpson, the janitor from her high school, used to push all day.

Derek stepped beside Rusty. "I got the water turned off. I'll start mopping."

"Thank you, son. The restoration company is on their way. Is your space okay?"

Derek nodded. "It seems to be fine. Don't worry about this. We'll take care of it. Her sales are increasing. We'll keep the momentum going."

Molly appreciated Derek's attempt to bring some light to the situation. But as she watched Rusty paddle his feet through the water, taking in the damage, she prepared herself.

"I think it might be time." The landlord's gaze dropped toward the ground.

Derek's brow crinkled. "But what about the time frame we discussed? I've implemented some new marketing strategies for Molly. I think they are working, but we need more time."

Molly cleared her throat. Or was she swallowing her pride? "Thank you, Derek, but as much as it pains me to say it, Rusty is right. Maybe I need to accept the fact that my store can't compete with the big guys." She paused, took in her surroundings and held out her hands to Rusty. "You mentioned you might not have to sell if my store does better. I know you want to retire with peace of mind that I'll be okay. I love you for that, but what happened this morning is a sign. It's time to cut my losses." Saying those words out loud spawned a queasiness deep in the pit of her stomach, one she hadn't felt since her mother passed away. She spun on her heel and headed toward her office.

"Wait!"

Molly stopped. Derek's tone meant business.

"I believe in this place. I believe in Book Buddies," he said to Molly. His cheeks flushed. "I believe in you." Turning his attention to Rusty, he continued. "You said you'd give me time to get Molly's store making a steady profit again. I can do that. I know I can."

"Wait, did you guys make some sort of deal?" Molly's eyes grazed over the two men.

Rusty nodded. "I promised your mother I'd look after you. This is about helping you and keeping my word to a special woman. That's all."

"It's true, Molly," Derek added. "We both have your best interest in mind. This is just a minor setback. Rusty, I'm asking you to keep your end of the bargain. I'll take care of the expenses involved in cleaning this place and any repairs. I promise it's going to be worth it. You can retire knowing Molly's store is thriving."

Molly's heart squeezed at Derek's words. As much as she didn't like the idea of him becoming her landlord, what other option did she have? Losing her store could mean losing Grace. She wouldn't allow that to happen. She'd have to keep her emotions out of it and look at things from a strictly business perspective. That's what she'd do in order to make a home for Grace.

Rusty placed his hand on Derek's shoulder. "Molly's mother would've liked you." He blew out a long breath. "I'll keep my word and give you time. But I can't let you pay for any repairs. This is still my property, so it's my responsibility." He removed his hand and extended it to Derek.

"Deal?"

"Yes, sir. It's a deal."

Rusty was right. Her mother would've loved Derek. But Molly had never told her mother Derek was the reason she'd been left at the altar. If she had, her mother would have told her to keep her distance. And that's what she planned to do. If there was any chance of Derek taking over as her landlord, it was all the more reason to keep her focus on business and her heart out of the equation.

* * *

Late Friday afternoon, Derek's phone chirped, pulling him from his laptop and the monthly budget he'd been working on for the past hour. A quick tap of the screen displayed an email notification from his bank. He bit down on his lower lip and read the correspondence. The loan he'd applied for was under further review. When he'd made his initial offer to Rusty, he hadn't foreseen any issues with getting approved for a loan. Now if it fell through, he wouldn't be able to afford his original offer, let alone the higher one to match eighty percent of the developer's bid. More waiting. Derek flopped back against his leather chair and looked at the ceiling.

The look on Molly's face yesterday morning had stuck in his mind. Her concern about the store flooding accounted for a fraction of her worries. What if she couldn't adopt Grace? Thankfully, the store would be easy to fix since there was no major water damage. The cleanup was almost done. Molly could open tomorrow. He doubted the adoption situation would be as simple if the store didn't start to turn a profit soon.

Derek skimmed over the remaining emails. He lifted his finger off the down arrow when he came upon the message from his mother. He'd opened and read it a couple of days ago, but he hadn't taken any action. His mother's suggestion to reach out to his father had been unexpected. He wasn't ready. Not yet. Maybe not ever.

A sudden burst of loud voices turned Derek's thoughts from his father. He saved his document and powered down the computer. He stepped outside his office and noticed of a group of patrons gathered at the front window of the shop.

"What's all of the commotion out there?" Derek walked toward Charles, who was busy grinding some coffee beans.

"Some of the hotshots from Mountain Ridge Development are out there casing out the town." Charles shook his head. "That can't be good."

Strange. From what Derek learned at the chamber of commerce meeting, this group wasn't supposed to arrive in Whispering Slopes until next week. What was their rush? "What makes you say that?"

Charles wiped his hands down the front of his apron. "I've seen this before. A quiet, quaint town gets bought out by some big-city company and everything changes. The little guy doesn't stand a chance."

Derek watched the three men dressed in expensive-looking suits. Their watches glistened in the sunlight while they strolled down the sidewalk, taking pictures and making notes on their iPads. They saw the potential. Like he'd seen the first time he'd come to check out Whispering Slopes. His jaw clenched, and he shook his head. "Well, I'm one of the little guys, and I'm not about to go down without a fight." His jaw loosened when he spotted Molly entering the store.

"What can I get you, Molly?" Charles called out when she moved toward the counter.

Derek's chest thumped, and her fruity scent teased his nose. "Hey, Molly."

She tucked a strand of hair behind her ear and narrowed her eyes in his direction. "Hey, Derek." She focused her attention back on Charles. "I'll have a tall latte with an extra shot of espresso."

"Whoa! Going for the hard stuff, huh?" Derek joked.

"I didn't get much sleep last night. I plan to work on my next newsletter, so I need the extra afternoon jolt."

Molly losing sleep over her situation wasn't a surprise. "Go have a seat over there." He pointed to the only empty table overlooking the main street through town.

She nodded, reached inside the pocket of her jeans and pulled out a credit card.

"No." With caution, he placed his hand over hers and allowed it to linger. "It's on the house."

A forced smile parted her pink lips before she headed across the store. No argument. She must be tired.

"Here you go, Derek. Take this and go on over there. Give her a reason to smile for real." Charles passed the steaming beverage over the counter.

With a million things flooding his mind, he approached Molly's table. There was so much he wanted to confess to her, like why on the day of her wedding, he'd told Ryan it was a mistake to get married. How his father's lies were the reason. More importantly, could he explain the emotions that had swirled through his mind the morning of the wedding? How devastated he'd been after learning about his father's indiscretion. Discovering his parents' marriage had been a lie and being the best man in his friend's wedding on the same day had been more than he could handle.

"A penny for your thoughts." Derek placed the coffee on the table in front of Molly and slid into the chair next to her.

She smiled. A real smile this time. "My mother used to say that."

"I'm in good company. Care to talk about it?"

Molly squeezed her eyes shut. When she opened them, a tear shimmered on her lower lid.

"Is it the store? Is that why you couldn't sleep last night?"

Her head shifted. The coffee grinder whirled. "It's part of the reason. At least the place has dried out, and I can open tomorrow morning."

Derek leaned closer. "So what kept you awake?"

Molly pressed her back against the chair. She wrapped her arms tightly around her chest.

The distress etched on Molly's face was undeniable. He didn't want to press her, so he remained quiet.

"When we were in college, you didn't know much about me. I mean, I was your best friend's girlfriend, but we never got to know each other."

That was true. He remembered little things about Molly, but he'd never made the time to learn more about her. Now he found himself questioning why. "I'm sorry. I should have made an effort to get to know you better."

"No, I'm sorry. I wasn't fishing for an apology. I was stating a fact. I didn't make a concerted effort to learn more about you, either." She turned her gaze downward. "I remember feeling like I was in a different class than you and Ryan."

"Why would you have thought that?"

Molly looked up. "You probably didn't know I was adopted."

"I think I remember Ryan mentioning it."

Molly leaned forward and rubbed her hands down her thighs. "I was abandoned by my birth mother and placed in foster care."

"I…um. I didn't know." Why hadn't Ryan mentioned that to him? Didn't best friends tell each other everything? He'd never even mentioned his doubts about marrying Molly. Then again, he always thought his parents were best friends, and look what happened with their relationship.

She shook her head. "You couldn't have known. I never told Ryan. He knew I was adopted, but not any of the details."

Derek cringed. More secrets. Just like his father. "But you were going to commit your life to him. Why didn't you want to share your past with him?" Secrets undermined trust. They were lies of omission. Marriages should be based on trust. This was exactly the reason committing his life to another person wasn't in the cards for him.

"When I met Ryan, he loved me in a way I'd never experienced." Molly raked her hands through her hair. "At least, at the beginning of our relationship. I was afraid if I told him about my past, he'd look at me like I was defective and no longer worthy of his love." She turned to Derek. Her eyes glistened with tears. "I was abused. What happened to me in some of the foster homes was degrading. I was ashamed and embarrassed to talk about it. For a long time, I believed I deserved it. My own birth mother didn't want me, so why would any of the foster families want to welcome me into their home and treat me like a child of their own?"

Derek's heart broke. He had no idea. Had Ryan calling off the wedding reopened old wounds for Molly? "I'm sorry you had to endure such a painful childhood, Molly. I hope you realize now what happened to you wasn't your fault."

She wiped a stray tear off her cheek.

Derek reached across the table and took her hand in his. "You were a defenseless child. I'm sorry you didn't have anyone to protect you." Having been raised in a loving home, Derek couldn't imagine how scared Molly must have been.

"It's the reason books are so important to me. They helped me to heal and took away the pain left behind from each bruise. The characters became my friends. I'd pretend I was part of their story, experiencing everything they did. Like working jigsaw puzzles, it was another way I escaped. Until recently, I believed the words and illustrations on those pages saved my life. But now I feel as though there's not a book in my store that can save me. Not only am I going to lose my store, but I'm going to lose my chance to save Grace. To make a home for her."

"Did someone harm Grace?" His fists tightened.

Molly nodded, and her face turned solemn. "Her file… When I read it… It was like revisiting my childhood. A place where I never wanted to return."

So this was why Grace appeared so withdrawn from others, why she seemed to come to life only when Duke was around. "That poor child. I'm so sorry."

"If I lose my store, there's no way the agency will allow me to continue with the adoption process. And if I don't come clean with Annie, it's only a matter of time before they learn I'm almost broke and a complete fraud."

Derek turned to the sound of deep voices entering his shop. It was the suits. Were they coming inside to case his storefront? He squared his shoulders and eyed the threesome as they moved across the store, tapping the screens of their iPads.

"There they are." Molly pointed to the group.

"Those are the people who are going to steal my dream. And maybe yours, too. You heard Rusty. They've got deep pockets."

Derek glanced at the men who had settled at a corner table. They were hunched over the screen held by the gray-haired senior of the group. Derek turned back to Molly. "I promise you, Molly, I won't let that happen. You won't lose your store or Grace."

Could he prevent it from happening? Was he filling her head with false hope? No. After learning about Molly's childhood and what Grace had experienced, he had no choice. He'd given Molly his word, and no matter what, he wouldn't follow in his father's footsteps and leave a trail of broken promises and shattered dreams.

Chapter Eleven

Molly stood in front of the full-length mirror in the corner of her bedroom. The floral print dress she'd worn to church earlier was now flung on her bed, along with a heap of other clothing. She was on her third outfit, yet still unable to decide what to wear. *It's only a picnic.* Why was she putting so much focus on how she looked? She knew why. Derek would be there with Duke. On Friday at his coffee shop, after she'd confessed her past to him, she couldn't get him out of her mind. This wasn't good. She needed to keep her focus on trying to build a relationship with Grace, not with Derek.

Three outfits later, dressed in black skinny jeans and a pink mock turtleneck sweater, Molly navigated the curved mountain road. The autumn leaves revealed golden yellows and fiery reds that reminded her of the upcoming Apple Harvest Festival. If things went well today, she could talk to Annie about taking Grace to the festival. Just the two of them... like mother and daughter.

As she cruised down Main Street, her eyes zoomed in on the three men in suits exiting Buser's General Store. The same gentlemen she and Derek had seen on Friday. Real estate wheeling and dealing must not take a day of rest.

Molly pulled into the empty loading zone outside the store. No deliveries were made on Sunday, so she could dash inside and grab some fried chicken. She placed the car in Park and exited the vehicle.

Like a giant bear hug, a warm sensation ignited her senses as she stepped inside the store. Molly had been coming to this place at least several times a week since she first moved to Whispering Slopes as a teenager.

"Hello, sweetie. Your chicken is almost ready." Elsie scurried from behind the counter and glided toward Molly with her arms wide open.

This was home. Aunt Elsie, the town, her store—she wasn't about to allow three men with fat wallets take it away. "Why were those guys in here, Auntie?"

"They're doing what they do. Snooping around

and trying to get some information from me." The elder woman reached to adjust her bun perched on the back of her head.

"What type of questions were they asking?" Molly didn't trust them. She'd done some sleuthing online and uncovered a few of their past development projects. They had a reputation of swooping into cozy and quaint towns and leaving behind overcrowded business districts with little affordable housing. Was this their plan for Whispering Slopes? Not on her watch.

"You know, the typical sniffing around kind."

Her auntie's nonchalant tone was a surprise. "Aren't you scared of what they might do to our town?" Since the chamber meeting, Molly had spent many hours imagining what could happen to the only home she'd ever known.

"Oh, fiddle-dee-dee. I've seen companies like this come and go over the years. Put your trust in the Lord, dear. He knows what's best for you and our town."

"But Rusty is considering selling, and the mayor seemed excited about the potential for growth in the town. At the meeting, I saw dollar signs in the eyes of some of the locals."

Elsie waved her hand. "There's not a person living in this town who doesn't come from a long line of Whispering Slope residents. They got excited by the prospect of big things coming to town, but in the end, people want to keep this area as it's always been. A welcoming and safe place to settle down and raise a family. A community where people do things for each other. You'll see. Trust me."

That's what Derek had said the other day. But trusting took courage and faith. After she was adopted by Shelley, Molly had started to believe in promises. Why had she stopped? "I hope you're right," Molly replied.

Elsie moved in closer. "Let's forget about all of this real estate mumbo jumbo. Today is a big day for you. You should be filled with joy, not worry."

It was important, but it also had her nerves rattled. What if Grace displayed the same lack of interest in getting to know her? Like the night Annie had brought her over for dessert and at Book Buddies. "I'm having a difficult time getting excited about the picnic. I'm afraid Grace won't like me."

"Why on earth would you think something like that? I don't know one person who's ever met you who didn't love you."

Molly couldn't shake the feeling, though. Grace could assume Molly would be like all of the others who'd opened their homes and given her hope only to be discarded like she was a worthless piece of garbage. Molly had grown up feeling like that until Shelley rescued her. She'd have to make Grace realize she wasn't the same as all of the other families. Molly wanted to make a home for Grace where she'd feel safe and loved.

"I appreciate you saying that, but I don't think it's going to be easy."

"Nothing worth having in life ever is easy, dear. Relax and be yourself today."

A beeper sounded from the kitchen in the back of the store. "There's your chicken. I'll be right back."

Molly watched as Elsie scurried off to package her meal. For a second, she was at ease. Her auntie had never steered her wrong in the past. Was it as simple as being herself? She glanced at her watch. She would soon find out.

Fifteen minutes later, Molly pulled her car into an empty parking spot at the park. She sucked in a deep breath and released it. *You can do this.* Her eyes scanned the area. A wooded path led to a grassy area filled with picnic tables and families enjoying a lazy Sunday afternoon. She exited her car and popped open the trunk to grab the food.

"It looks like we are both running behind."

Molly jumped at the familiar deep voice. She turned with a firm grip on the basket Elsie had loaded with chicken, potato salad, freshly baked rolls and half a German chocolate cake. Elsie knew it was Molly's favorite. "Derek. You startled me."

He flashed a smile, and her heart fluttered. "I'm sorry. I thought you saw me. Here, let me take it." Derek reached for the basket and held Duke's leash with his other hand. The dog let out a whimper. "I think Duke smells fried chicken. Is he right?" The dog wove between their legs with his nose in the air.

"It's not just any chicken. It's the best you'll taste in the valley. Aunt Elsie has quite the reputation for frying the crispiest bird you'll ever have." Molly dipped and scratched the top of Duke's head. He responded with a wet, sloppy kiss on the hand.

"I think he likes you," Derek remarked.

"I hope Grace feels the same today." Molly closed the trunk.

Derek playfully bumped his shoulder against Molly. "Relax. It's a gorgeous day. You're going to have a great time with Grace."

The couple moved down the path with Duke's nose to the ground and his tail whipping from side to side.

Derek laughed. "Duke loves to be out with people."

At the end of the path, Molly's eyes moved

from table to table in search of Grace. Seconds passed, and her heart squeezed at the sight of the golden hair glistening in the afternoon sunlight peeking through the towering trees.

Duke released a bark, and Grace turned. Molly watched as the little girl's eyes ignited with joy. She sprang from the table where she sat next to Annie and ran across the open field.

"Duke!"

The dog's excitement increased, and Derek's arm was almost pulled from its socket.

"Whoa, boy. Hang on a second," Derek commanded, struggling to hold on to the leash.

Molly's heart sank as the child dropped to her knees and threw her arms around Duke. She longed for such a greeting from Grace, but she knew it would take time. Or would it never happen?

"Duke sure is happy to see you, Grace. I think he remembers you." Derek eyed Molly.

"I'm so happy you brought him with you, Mr. Derek." The child beamed at Derek as Duke flopped on the ground and rolled over for a good belly rub.

Molly felt like the last kid picked for the softball team. Grace hadn't once looked in her direction.

Derek peered at Molly. He understood her

disappointment. "I hope you like chicken. Miss Molly has a basket full."

"Hi, Grace. It's nice to see you again." Molly stepped closer to the child.

Grace glanced at the basket but didn't look toward Molly. Instead, she turned the conversation back to Derek. "Does Duke like chicken, Mr. Derek?"

Molly turned, head down, and walked toward Annie's table.

"Hey, Molly. It's a perfect day for a picnic, isn't it?" Annie stood and hugged Molly's stiff frame before stepping back. "What's wrong?"

"It wasn't my imagination the other night." Molly looked toward the child as she and Derek wrestled with Duke.

"What about the other evening?"

"With Grace. It's official. She doesn't like me."

Annie chuckled. "You're being silly. She hasn't had a chance to get to know you."

Grace squealed, confirming Molly's beliefs. The child didn't want to get to know her. "She doesn't know Derek, but look at them." She pointed to the two giggling as Grace fed Duke a dog treat.

"Give it time, Molly."

That was the thing. She was running out of time. If sales didn't increase soon at her bookstore, Rusty was going to sell. The clock was ticking. It was only a matter of time before Annie learned how dire her financial situation was. Wouldn't it be best if she heard it straight from Molly and not on a bank statement?

"Are you okay?" Annie questioned.

"Not really. There's something you need to know before we move forward with the adoption process."

Annie tilted her head. "You've changed your mind?"

"Oh no, of course not. There's nothing I want more in the world than to open my home and heart to that little girl." Molly paused and directed her attention back to Grace and Derek. "But I need to be honest with you. My store is in trouble. I'm doing everything possible to save it, but there's a chance I might have to close the doors."

Annie reached over and rested her hand on Molly's arm. "Oh, sweetie, I'm so sorry to hear this. I love your shop. It's such a tremendous asset to our community. What can I do to help?"

Molly's breath hitched. "That's kind. I'm not sure what else can be done. Derek has designed a website for me and also did the makeover on the store."

"And it looks great. It sure was nice of him." Annie winked.

"It's not what you think. There's nothing happening between us. This is all business." It had to be. She couldn't allow it to be anything more. No way.

"I'm not so sure it's all business for Derek. I've noticed the way he looks at you," Annie said.

A mother and a teenage daughter strolled past the table. Holding hands, they laughed and whispered like best friends. Molly's heart squeezed. She pulled her focus away to ease the pain. "Trust me. I'm nothing more than a stepping stone for him to expand his franchise."

"If you say so."

Molly squared her shoulders. "I know so. Anyway, my bank balance doesn't look like I can support a child, but I'm asking for time."

"I appreciate your honesty. We've dealt with this before, so try not to worry. I'll explain your situation to my supervisor. I'm sure we can continue to move forward and just allow you the time you need to work through your financial difficulties."

But what if she couldn't? If she was forced to sell, how would she make a living? How would she ever be in a position to adopt Grace? Wasn't it unfair to Grace to get her hopes up?

Derek kept telling her not to quit. Not to give up. Was he right? She watched Derek and

Grace stroll across the grassy field with Duke traipsing beside them. Grace's giggles filled the air. The child looked at Derek, smiled and reached for his hand. Molly's stomach rolled as doubt and uncertainty rocked her to the core. Reality hit like a migraine headache. Derek was once again stealing her dream.

Warning sirens erupted in Derek's head. What just happened? Why was this tiny hand inside his creating a firestorm of emotions he couldn't identify? The glaring look Molly shot his way extinguished the warmth, and he pulled his hand away. "Why don't you go sit next to Miss Molly, Grace?"

The child pouted with her lower lip out. This picnic wasn't getting off to a good start. Three females in his proximity, and he'd already upset two of them.

Grace hopped on the bench. Her eyes remained focused on Duke, who had settled into a shady spot in the grass. The scent of pine drifted on a breeze.

Annie directed her attention to Grace. "Did you enjoy yourself at Miss Molly's Book Buddies the other day?"

Derek was pleased Annie was trying to engage Molly and Grace in a conversation. How could they ever get to know each other if they didn't talk?

Grace nodded her head. "Uh-huh."

Annie fired off another question. "What did you like the best?"

"I liked seeing Mr. Derek and Duke the best."

Ouch. Not exactly the answer any of the adults had hoped for—especially not Molly. He noticed the disappointment on her face. An awkward silence hung in the air.

Molly sat taller. "Grace, do you like fried chicken?" She opened the wicker basket and pulled out a stack of foam plates with three divided compartments.

"Yes," the child whispered.

"It smells delicious." Annie took the plates and put one in front of each of the adults and Grace.

Grace leaned across the table toward Derek. "What about Duke? Doesn't he get a piece of chicken?"

Derek smiled. "Oh no, he's a vegetarian."

Grace covered her mouth and giggled. "Dogs don't eat vegetables."

"But rabbits do," Molly added. "I once had a pet rabbit. I used to feed him carrots."

Grace frowned at Molly. "Rabbit shouldn't be kept in cages. They need to run free. I don't like animals to be locked in cages."

Derek eyed Molly, who had abruptly turned her focus back to the basket of food, her face red.

"I'm sure Miss Molly let her rabbit play outside of its cage. Didn't you?"

Grace looked at Molly and back to Derek. "Can me and you take Duke on a hike after we eat?" she asked.

Molly sat stiffly, wearing an empty stare. Poor Molly. This was getting more uncomfortable by the minute. He knew how important it was for her to form a bond with Grace. Her struggles with her store were hard enough. She couldn't be rejected by Grace on top of everything else. "I think it might be a better idea if you and Miss Molly go together. Duke might be ready for a break from me. I'm sure he gets tired of hanging out with me all the time." He winked at Molly, who remained silent.

"That's a great idea," Annie chimed in, and passed out the paper cups. "I wanted to talk to you about your coffee franchise, Derek. My sister and brother-in-law are considering opening one in Dallas."

Derek had a sneaky feeling Annie was trying to think of an excuse for Molly and Grace to have some alone time together. Molly would be brokenhearted if the day passed without her making a connection with Grace. "I'd be happy to answer any questions. But first, let's eat. I'm so hungry I could eat a hippopotamus."

Grace giggled and bit into the chicken leg Molly had placed on her plate. "You're funny, Mr. Derek."

Derek considered Molly and Grace as they sat side by side, yet worlds apart. Still, with what Molly had shared about her own upbringing, along with Grace's experience in foster care, they might soon discover they had a lot in common. As tragic as it was, could the commonality create a bond? He continued to watch Molly and Grace listen to Annie talk about her new kitten. Then reality hit. The sooner he stopped picturing Molly, Grace and himself as a family, the less likely he'd risk getting hurt down the road. But these thoughts continued to cling like a load of clothes fresh out of the dryer.

Chapter Twelve

Grace was avoiding her.

Molly realized it the moment she, Grace and Duke left Derek and Annie talking at the picnic table. There had been some small talk during the meal, but Annie had done most of the talking. Molly had hoped once they were alone, Grace would come around. Now, as they tramped down the mud-caked path, the only sounds were leaves crunching underneath their feet, birds singing in the towering red oaks and Duke's panting. This was not going as she'd planned.

The three moved down the path at a brisk pace set by the dog. Twigs kicked up underneath his paws.

"Duke, slow down. You're going to pull Grace's arm out of its socket." Molly's plea fell on deaf ears as Duke's nose worked its way through the wild flowers camped along the trail.

Water rushing over the rocks echoed through the trees. Grace's red tennis shoes came to an abrupt stop as they got closer to the river. Duke whimpered.

Molly stopped and looked down at the child, who stood frozen. "What is it, Grace? Don't you want to see the river?"

Grace remained silent, but she shook her head in sharp, rapid movements.

"I thought Duke would like to splash in the water along the shoreline," Molly said, hoping to convince Grace to continue with their hike. She didn't want their time to end. They'd hardly spoken three words to each other. Like her store, she was running out of time with the child. If she didn't have a breakthrough with Grace soon, Annie would be forced to look for another home for the child.

Duke barked and lunged forward. He wanted to swim.

"Are you sure you don't want to keep going?" Molly hoped she'd have a change of heart.

Grace jumped when overhead, a large black crow took flight, its wings flapping.

Molly's heart broke. Something or someone had instilled fear into this child. If only she could get Grace to talk, perhaps she could help her.

"I want to go see Mr. Derek." Grace turned and Duke followed. They trudged up the path. Molly had lost her chance—again. More confused than ever, she questioned whether adopting Grace was truly in God's plan for her life.

Wednesday afternoon, behind the register, Molly nibbled on a peanut butter sandwich.

"I've never known anyone who eats a peanut butter sandwich without jelly." Caitlin eyed Molly's lunch. "Doesn't it get stuck in your throat?"

Molly lifted her bottle of water and took a long swig. "Not when you have something to wash it down with." She tapped her iPad, opening a new email. "Hey, look, we already have five hundred subscribers to the newsletter."

Caitlin opened the box of office supplies that had been delivered earlier that morning. "That sounds promising." She paused and glanced around the empty store. "I wonder where everyone is?"

"We had some customers earlier this morning, but you know Wednesdays are often slow. It's why I decided it would be the best day for Book Buddies." True, midweek was normally quiet, but this place was dead today. She hoped there would be a full house later.

The front door chimed. Finally, a customer. Molly pulled her eyes away from the device and spotted Derek.

"Hey, ladies." He paused and looked around the store. "Boy, you'd never know you had a flood in here a few days ago." He flashed a smile.

Molly's heart fluttered. Wait. There would be no fluttering heart today. Or any day. Molly fingered through the stack of papers resting on the counter in front of her, willing the unexpected feelings to take a hike. But what was it she was feeling? These emotions had gnawed at her since the picnic on Sunday. Derek's interaction with Grace had triggered something inside, but it wasn't only jealousy. She couldn't help but think Derek would make a good father.

"Hey, Mr. McKinney. Thanks again for speaking to my marketing class on Monday. My classmates are still buzzing about it. You inspired a lot of people." Caitlin smiled, removing the reams of copy paper from the box.

"It was my pleasure. It's great to see so much entrepreneurial spirit in young people."

Caitlin smiled. "Yeah, I think everyone wants to be their own boss."

Lately, Molly didn't believe being your own

boss was as great as it sounded. She used to, but these days, not so much.

"I'm going to take the rest of these supplies to the back. Thanks again, Mr. McKinney." Caitlin scooped the box up and scurried out of the room.

Molly turned to Derek. "It was nice of you to speak to Caitlin's class."

"I was happy to do it."

Molly considered Derek's words. She admired the humility he had despite his success. He didn't boast about his achievements. He went out into the community to share his wisdom and help others. No matter her feelings about the past, she had to admit that he was a good man. "So, what's this?" She pointed to the blue sheet of paper in his hands.

Derek placed the item in front of her. Molly took notice of her store's logo at the top of the page.

"What do you think?" Derek asked.

Molly rubbed her eyes. Her insides vibrated. "Is this for real?"

Derek nodded.

"Mark Potter is coming here?" Molly had been a fan of his work for years. As a best-selling mystery writer, the man knew how to weave a story that kept readers on the edge of their seats. She'd had many sleepless nights reading his novels. "How in the world did you manage to convince Mark Potter to come to my little store for a book signing? This can't be happening."

"Yes, Mark has agreed to come to your shop a week from this Friday."

Molly felt like a marionette who'd had its strings cut. She clutched the side of the counter to keep her balance. "I'm sorry, but I'm having a difficult time wrapping my head around all of this."

Derek reached for her arm. "Let's go sit down at the table before you fall and injure yourself." He laughed.

Molly made it to the table. Authors like Mark Potter didn't make appearances at small stores. She'd seen his book tour schedule. He always hit the big chain bookstores. She slid into the cushioned chair. Derek sat down beside her.

"How is this happening?" When she'd thought about hosting an author book signing, she'd never dreamed of having a writer with his reputation. "He's so famous. How did he end up in Whispering Slopes?"

"I met Mark when I opened my first coffee shop in Washington, DC. I was a big fan of his books, so when he started coming into my store to write each day, I was thrilled. It wasn't long before every aspiring writer in the area gathered to write and drink coffee. I guess they believed if they wrote where Mark was working, they could create a bestseller, too. Or maybe they thought there was something in the coffee. Anyway, since he wrote five hours a day, five days a week, he and I became pretty good friends."

Molly couldn't imagine having a writer like Mark coming to her store each day to pen their next novel. "You keep in touch with him?"

"Yeah. He still writes in my shop. We email or text a couple of times a month. That's how I found out he's going to be in the area. He's completing his recent book tour."

"Yes, I read about it." Molly didn't want to admit it, but when she'd gotten the writing bug, she'd started stalking writers on social media. One of her favorite things to do was peruse author websites and read about their road to publication. "I saw his schedule. I was surprised he wasn't making a stop at my competition."

Derek nodded. "He does appear at some of the larger chain stores, but he prefers the smaller shops. He knows it's difficult to compete with the big guys. He called me after he saw your website."

Molly's head was spinning. "Mark Potter saw my store online?"

"Yes, he did. He asked if I knew the owner, and if you ever hosted book signings."

"So this is real? It's going to happen?" She reached for the flyer Derek had created and brushed away a tear.

"Hey, don't cry." He took her hand and gave it a quick squeeze. "This is supposed to be good news. It could be a big deal for your store, Mols."

A tingling sensation in her arm caught her off guard, and Molly pulled her hand free. "I don't know how to thank you, Derek. You've already done so much to help me, but this… I can't believe it." She scanned her shop. Could this be the game changer for her business?

"I haven't told you the best part." Derek leaned back against his chair.

"You mean there's more?" Molly turned to a group of vivacious teenagers who entered the shop.

"Welcome to Bound to Please Reads," Caitlin called out from behind the register. "Let us know if we can help you find anything."

Molly smiled. She was blessed to have Caitlin working for her. One day, she hoped she could afford to hire her as a real employee rather than a volunteer. Caitlin had expressed her dream of owning a bookstore. Of course, with Molly's declining sales, she might change her mind. Another reason Molly couldn't fail. She wanted to inspire young people, not crush their dreams.

Molly gazed in Derek's direction. "You've done so much already. Look at the time you've spent remodeling my store, plus the social media work, all while opening your own store."

"I'm blessed. With each new store I open, they seem to run themselves. Besides, Charles and Nell have everything under control. I think they like it better when I'm not there." He joked.

"Still, I don't know how I can ever repay you."

"It's not necessary. Please, let me get back to the best part. Mark and I did some brainstorming on how to help bump up your sales. He's going to give away autographed copies of his latest book to people who attend the signing at your store."

Molly listened and tried to absorb Derek's words. "That's generous of him, but I'm not quite understanding how it will help my sales."

A smile spread across Derek's face. "Remember that you had a jump in business when I offered the coupon at my store to customers who made a purchase at your shop?"

That was true. She had seen a spike in profits from the coupon, but it hadn't been enough to dig her out of debt. "Yes, I remember."

"Well, Mark's going to give away signed copies, but the customer must first present a receipt for a purchase from your bookstore. I thought maybe we could have a ten-dollar minimum."

Molly's pulse raced. "I can't believe he's offered to do this."

"He's always been a huge supporter of independent bookstores. He says they are the ones who launched his career. He's excited to help you."

Could this be the answer to her prayers? Would having a famous author in her store make it possible for her to get out of debt and to move forward with her plans to adopt Grace? As she studied Derek, the man who was doing everything in his power to help her, she still couldn't shake away the pain he'd caused her in the past. If it weren't for Derek, would she be living a happily married life with children?

Derek leaned in closer. "This is important to me. Not only because your success can impact my own, but I feel responsible for what happened two years ago. I need to tell you about the day of the wedding."

The sounds in the store became muffled. Like someone had stuffed cotton balls deep inside her ears. The teenagers' voices were garbled. The feelings of abandonment she'd experienced as a child, and had struggled to keep locked away as an adult, plowed into her as they had the day of her wedding. Derek had ruined everything on what should've been the happiest day of her life.

"I think you better leave. I really need to keep my focus on my store. And going forward, I'd like for you to honor my request about keeping our interaction strictly business. No more discussions about the past."

"But I'd like to explain," he pleaded.

Molly pushed away from the table. Her chair screeched across the tile. With lightning speed, she moved toward her office and didn't look back at the man who'd destroyed her future.

The following Tuesday, Derek stepped out of the First National Valley Bank. The afternoon sun stole his sight for a moment. He removed the dark sunglasses perched on his head and slid them over his eyes. The meeting with the loan officer hadn't gone as he'd hoped. He'd been approved for a loan, but it wasn't enough to put him in a position to outbid the investor who had interest in Rusty's property, even with the discount Rusty had offered. He needed another plan. But what? If Mark's visit to Molly's store didn't generate enough revenue, he wouldn't be able to fulfill the promise he'd made to Rusty. She'd be forced to close, and the property could be turned into office space. The landscape of the town would be forever changed.

Derek moved down the sidewalk toward his store as the sun dipped behind the distant evergreens. Swaths of light pink and purple began to take over the sky. Thoughts of Molly filled his head. He couldn't stop thinking that he was the reason Molly had been abandoned for a second time in her life. He needed to explain his reasons for having the conversation with Ryan, but Molly had managed to avoid him since their conversation last Wednesday. After he'd left her store, he'd kept his nose to the window and had been relieved to see Annie had brought Grace to Book Buddies. Derek hoped Molly had made some progress in building a relationship with her.

"At least two hours? Okay, thank you. Goodbye."

Derek turned to the familiar voice. His breath hitched when he spotted Molly standing next to her VW Bug with the hood raised. She stood with one hand on her phone and the other clutching the back of her head while her red hair flowed over her shoulders.

"Can I help?" Derek approached with caution, hesitant to cross the boundary she'd established.

A truck whizzed past, causing a breeze to lift her hair off her shoulders. "If you know anything about cars, I suppose you could. It won't start. My Check Engine light came on while I was driving to work this morning. When I pulled around from the back lot to go home for the day, the car made a strange noise before it conked out." Molly slammed the hood, rounded the vehicle and brushed her hands down her gray pants.

She was cute when she got frustrated. "Hmm, I'm better with flat tires and dead batteries. That light has always been a mystery to me."

Molly half laughed.

This was a good sign. "So you've got a bit of a wait before someone can come and check it out?"

"At least two hours. This is a small town. How many broken-down cars could there be?" She glanced at her watch. "I was ready to go home, have some dinner and curl up with a good book."

"Oh, so you had one of those days, too, huh?" After the disappointing news about the loan, Derek was looking forward to calling it a day himself. But he was starving and ready for some dinner. He couldn't think of any better company than Molly. "Since we're both hungry, why don't we go get something to eat?"

Molly scuffed her shoe along the pavement. "I don't think that's such a good idea, Derek."

"I know you said business only, but we do need to talk about the book signing on Friday. Plus, we both have to eat dinner."

Molly looked around and placed her hand to her stomach. "Well, I am pretty hungry. I didn't have time for lunch. Believe it or not, the store was busy today."

"That's great to hear. It was probably the captivating newsletter you sent that drew in the crowds. By the way, it was a great idea to start twenty-percent-off Tuesday."

Molly blushed. "You read my newsletter?"

"Of course I did. What do you say we grab a bite, take a walk around the lake afterward, and discuss business? The temperature is perfect." He swung his arm out, hoping she'd lead the way.

"I can't go too far. What if they come early?" Her brow crinkled.

Derek laughed. "When have you ever known an emergency road service to arrive on time, much less early? You won't miss them. The place I have in mind is a short walk from here."

Molly nodded. "Let me run inside and grab a sweater."

Derek waited while Molly entered her shop. She'd been right to decide their relationship needed to stay professional. His time was running out. The last thing he needed was to make any emotional connections in Whispering Slopes. He'd come here for business only.

Chapter Thirteen

Molly stepped inside her store, closed the door and exhaled. The hairs on the back of her neck tingled. Her heart pounded despite the distance from Derek. She had to get a grip. Yes, he was gorgeous, but she couldn't fall for him. She wouldn't.

She snuck a quick backward glance outside. Derek stood leaning against a lamppost with his hands in the front pockets of his black jeans. *Stop staring at him.* Squaring her shoulders, she headed to the back of the store to grab her sweater and turn off the lights in her office.

Moments later, with the alarm armed, she turned the key in the door and twirled around to find Derek standing inches from her. He smelled like her favorite cinnamon candle she loved to burn during the holidays.

"All set?" He flashed a smile that could melt

a popsicle in the middle of winter. Her heart accelerated for the second time in the past ten minutes. This needed to stop. Keeping things professional meant all matters of the heart had to be kept under wraps. Derek was the reason her heart had been broken two years ago. There was no way she'd allow him a repeat performance. She'd have to make sure they kept the conversation on the book signing.

"Sure. Let's go."

The couple made their way down the sidewalk that snaked through downtown. One by one, the street lights overhead flickered on as the businesses closed for the day.

"I'm still getting used to things closing down so early," Derek commented as they rounded a corner. "It's nice to watch the town go to sleep for the night."

"Everyone likes to get home to have dinner as a family. It's one of the things I love about this town." Molly dreamed of the day she'd cook dinner for her family. Of course, it could be years if her circumstances didn't change in a hurry. She'd been on edge waiting to hear from Annie about her request to take Grace to the Apple Harvest Festival.

"Family is important to you, isn't it?" Derek asked.

Her heart squeezed. She couldn't deny it

wasn't something she desperately wanted. "Yes. Isn't it to you?"

Derek stopped in his tracks and faced her. "Can I answer after we get our food?" He pointed toward the man-made lake next to the town's only roundabout. "I discovered a great food truck over there. They've got the best chili."

"Sounds good to me." Molly was surprised he didn't answer her question with a simple yes. In college, she'd gotten the impression Derek had a close relationship with his family.

The spicy aroma tickled Molly's nose as they neared the truck. "Yum. It smells so good."

"What can I get you? Mild, spicy or pass the fire hose?" Derek laughed.

"I'm up for the challenge. Pass the hose."

"That's my girl." He glanced over his shoulder. "Do you want to grab a table?" He nodded toward the empty seats closest to the water.

"Sure." Molly moved toward the table. The full moon shimmered over the lake, igniting it with a glow like thousands of twinkle lights. She took a seat on the bench. Gentle waves splashed ashore, filling the air with a soothing melody.

Derek moved toward her carrying a tray with two bowls of chili and three beverages. Her pulse increased when a smile flashed across his face, drawing her attention to his smooth, chiseled features, broad shoulders and slim hips.

Stop staring. You're here to discuss the book signing on Friday. With speed, she shifted her gaze away.

"I got you an extra water, just in case." He placed the tray of food on the table and slid onto the cedar seat facing her.

Molly reached for a plastic spoon and leaned toward the bowl. "It certainly looks delicious."

"Try it." Derek scooped a heaping portion and gulped down a bite. "It's the best."

Molly spooned a portion and popped it in her mouth. The velvety consistency contained a perfect balance of sweet and spicy. "Oh my! This is the best chili I've ever eaten." She took another bite. Within a second, her mouth ignited into a fiery inferno. Jalapeño. Lots of jalapeños. Her eyes began to water.

"Are you okay over there?"

Through her blurry eyes, Molly reached for a drink, but the cup tipped over. Water splashed in all directions, but most of it went on Derek. She snatched the second cup and downed half of its contents before her eyes locked with her dinner companion's. "Sorry. Usually I can handle jalapeños."

He sheepishly looked down. "Oh, maybe it's the cayenne pepper, too." He grabbed a napkin to clean up the spill before he spooned in a mouthful. "I can't get enough of this stuff."

Molly drained the remaining water and placed the empty cup on the table. "You must have a mouth made of steel." How in the world could he eat it so fast? He was halfway through his bowl. "Don't get me wrong, the chili is incredible, but it sure packs a punch."

"I learned the hard way. Now I order the medium fire. It's plenty hot enough for the average person." He smiled before passing his water across the table. "I think you need this more than I do."

She accepted his offer and downed the liquid in four large gulps. "You could have at least told me." She crumpled her napkin and playfully tossed it at his head.

He ducked, bent over and grabbed the trash. "I assumed the phrase 'pass the fire extinguisher' would give you a pretty good hint."

Molly laughed. "I guess you're right." She spooned out half as much as her previous bite and ate it. "It is the best chili I've ever tasted, but you need to eat it slowly."

Derek rested one elbow on top of the table and placed his fist underneath his chin. He leaned in closer. "You're a tough woman."

Molly shrugged. "I'm not sure I agree with you."

A light breeze kicked up, carrying the chirping of crickets.

Derek looked around. "That sound always reminds me of going back to school in the fall."

"What's that?"

"Crickets. When I was a kid, I remember lying in bed the night before the first day of school. I'd toss and turn while the crickets sang outside my window. I never liked to see summer come to an end. Do you remember hearing them?"

Molly shivered. "No. Most of the time, the crickets were drowned out by the adults in the house screaming and yelling. With the exception of one family, most of the people who fostered me weren't the most upstanding citizens."

Her mind drifted to Grace, and a chill ran down her spine. The past two nights, she'd woken in the early morning hours, unable to breathe. Each time, she'd had a dream Grace had fallen into the river after they'd spent the afternoon together laughing and sharing secrets. In the dream, Molly tried to reach Grace as the child struggled to hold on to a tree branch hanging low over the water. Both nights, Molly's eyes flew open as Grace lost her grip and was swept away. Molly couldn't save her in her dream, but this wasn't a dream. The adoption was real.

"I'm sorry to rouse bad memories." Derek picked at a napkin.

She rolled one shoulder and then the other. "It's okay. It was a long time ago. Boy, my childhood must seem like a nightmare compared to yours."

"Is that why you asked if I wanted a family? Because you believe mine was so perfect when I was young?" Derek's left brow arched.

"I know you said talking about your family is off-limits, but you had parents who loved and nurtured you. It's what every kid should have." Molly wiped a stray tear. "It's what I want for Grace."

Silence hung in the space between them. Derek looked to the sky before turning his focus to Molly. "It was all a lie."

Molly was confused. From what she knew through Ryan, Derek had a family life most kids would dream of having. "I'm not sure I understand what you mean."

Derek took the plastic spoon and stirred the almost empty bowl. "My family wasn't as it appeared to the outside world." He laughed, dropping the spoon and raking his hand through his hair. "It wasn't as it appeared to me, either."

The distraught look on Derek's face was unnerving. His personality was always upbeat and positive, but since the conversation had turned to his family, his mood had darkened. "Do you want to talk about it? If it's too painful, I understand."

"No, I've wanted to talk about it." Color drained from Derek's face. "Because this lie affected you, too."

Molly had no idea where Derek was going with this conversation, and a part of her wasn't sure she wanted to know. How could his family have any effect on her? She pulled in a deep breath and slowly exhaled. "What is it, Derek?"

"When I was a little boy, I wanted to be like my father. He'd wake early every morning and head out to work, often before sunrise. He dressed in expensive suits and carried a shiny black leather briefcase. On most nights, he didn't come home until after my mother and I had eaten dinner. It wasn't until I got older that I understood what he did for a living."

"Ryan told me he was a banker."

Derek nodded. "Yes. He worked as a loan officer, handling multimillion-dollar accounts. On those rare nights when he got home in time for dinner, it felt like Christmas to me. I wanted to spend as much time with him as possible." He stopped and took a drink from the cup of water in the middle of the table.

"And did you?" Molly was afraid she knew the answer.

Derek's shoulders drooped, and he shook his head. "Not as much as I would've liked to. As a young boy, my mother tried to explain that he was a busy man, but I didn't understand. My father was my hero. I wanted to hang out with him. I wanted him to love me."

Molly's heart ached for that little boy.

"As I got older, I realized a lot of responsibility came with my father's job. I accepted the fact that our family vacations often consisted of my mother and me jetting off somewhere alone. My father would join us later for a day or two—never longer."

Derek looked out toward the lake. His eyes pooled with pain.

"I'm sorry you weren't able to spend time with him, Derek. Maybe it was important to him to be a good provider and give his family a comfortable life." It may have been the case, although Molly was still confused about the lie and how it impacted her. But she didn't want to push him, so she focused her attention toward the water, as well.

After a few moments of silence, Derek rose to his feet. He removed the empty food containers from the table. Molly watched as he meandered to a nearby trash can and disposed of the garbage. He turned, moved toward her and made a weak attempt at a smile. "Do you want to go for a walk around the lake?" He extended his hand to her.

Molly's and Derek's hands coupled, and he helped her to her feet. A wave of light-headedness took hold. Her legs wobbled as they continued to move toward the water. If she were truthful to herself, she'd have to admit Derek's touch was nice. It felt safe and warm. This couldn't be good. Could it?

Overhead, the full moon streamed light on the dirt path leading to the lake, and Derek kept a firm hold on Molly's hand. He told himself it was so she wouldn't trip on a stick and fall. Yeah, right. He liked it. He liked it a lot. This wasn't supposed to happen. Once he shared his family secret and how it played a role in ruining her wedding day, he might never feel the warmth of her touch again. But it was a chance he had to take. She deserved to know the entire truth of that day.

They stepped onto the cement sidewalk that zigzagged along the lake. Ahead, a young couple walked with their arms locked.

"Look, they have paddle boats." Derek pointed to the row of boats moored along the dock. "You could bring Grace and have some time alone on the lake."

"I don't know. When we were on the picnic, I got the impression she isn't a fan of the water. I do hope to take Grace to the Apple Harvest Festival on Saturday. Annie's been great about giving me time to get my financial situation back on track. She believes in my store."

"As do I," Derek said.

"Thanks. If the book signing goes well, there's a chance I can begin to claw my way out of debt."

Yesterday, Derek had spoken with Mark about the event and offered his guest room so the author wouldn't have to deal with booking a hotel room. He planned to arrive in town Thursday evening. "Speaking of the book signing, Mark called me yesterday."

Molly stopped walking and looked at Derek. "I hope it's not bad news."

"On the contrary. Mark spoke with his publisher and explained your situation. Since they like to support independent bookstores, they're donating another thousand books to sign at your store."

Molly's mouth fell open. She pivoted and threw her arms around him in a tight hug. "I can't believe this! Thank you so much, Derek." She lifted her head off of his shoulder, and their eyes locked. Her breath smelled sweet against his face. If he moved just the slightest bit, their lips would touch. Is that what she wanted? He pulled back. "You're welcome, but it was mainly Mark's idea."

Molly furrowed her brow. "But you orchestrated all of it. If it weren't for you, Mark wouldn't be coming to my store."

"Please, don't make me out to be a hero." He stepped back and stuffed his hands in his pockets.

"What is it? Is this about the lie you mentioned back at the table? Please, tell me what's going on." Molly moved toward him and rested her hand on his forearm.

Now was his chance. He'd waited long enough. "Let's sit." He guided her to a bench with a view of the water. Molly took a seat first, and Derek settled in beside her. He sucked in a slow breath and released it. "You have every reason to hate me. The day of your wedding— Ryan changed his mind about marrying you because of what I said to him."

"Is that why you brought me here? To tell me what you said?" she asked with her gaze focused on the lake.

"I told him he was making a mistake."

Derek watched Molly. Her eyes glazed over as she attempted to process what he'd told her.

"I heard what you said. That day… I over-heard you and Ryan talking."

Derek's stomach knotted. "You what? Where?"

"At the church. I was heading to the rest-room before the ceremony started. I passed by the nursery, the door was ajar, and I heard the two of you talking. You told Ryan he shouldn't marry me." She raked her hand through her hair. The moon spotlighted the tears glistening in the corners of her eyes. His heart twisted. If only he could do it all over again. But would he have handled things differently? Would he have held his peace? He'd been so upset that day, he doubted it.

"For the past two years, I've tried to under-stand why you would do something so harsh. And why Ryan would have listened to you. I never did anything to you to justify such cru-elty."

"What else did you hear?"

"Nothing. I didn't need to hear any more. I never heard Ryan's voice again except for when he whispered in my ear that he couldn't marry me." Tears raced down Molly's face. "I'd been abandoned again, but this time in front of the entire congregation."

"There's more to the story, Molly. It's not an excuse, but maybe it will help you to under-stand why I said what I did to Ryan." He blew out a strong breath. "The morning of your wedding, I found out my father had another life."

Molly placed her hand on the base of her neck. "What do you mean?"

Besides Ryan and Mark, Derek had never shared this secret with anyone. For some foolish reason, he believed not talking about it would mean it wasn't real. But he knew the truth. There was no point in trying to hide it any longer. "As a child, my father preached the importance of family. It was the only thing that mattered in this world. And he said keeping my word was the most important virtue I could ever have." Recalling his father's falsehoods made him sick to his stomach. "But I'll tell you a family secret. That man, my father—he had another family."

They sat shoulder to shoulder while insects buzzed in the night air. Derek considered Molly. Her shimmering emerald eyes blinked in rapid succession. It was a lot to digest. It had been two years, and there were times Derek was still unable to process the fact that his life would never be the same. "I know. It's hard to believe. It's like something from a made-for-television movie." Derek dropped his focus to the ground.

"I'm sorry. I'm not sure what to say. It's so

unbelievable." Molly leaned forward and turned to him. "Ryan never mentioned it."

On the day of the wedding, Ryan had laughed when Derek told him about his father. He'd thought Derek was joking. Sadly, it was no joke. "That's because Ryan didn't know until the day of the wedding. And he made a promise to me that he'd never tell anyone. He said it wasn't his secret to share." Despite the cool, crisp air, perspiration crossed his brow. He ran the back of his hand across his forehead and blew out a breath. "I'd forgotten how hard this is to talk about."

Molly placed her hand on his shoulder. "If it's too difficult, you don't have to say any more."

Since his father's confession, he'd felt as though he were living inside a pressure cooker. The time was right for Molly to know the entire truth of that day. "No, I need to talk about this."

"Fair enough."

Derek leaned back and pressed his shoulders against the bench. The day was seared into his brain. "The morning of your wedding, I was running late. I'd forgotten to pick up my tuxedo at the cleaners. My father had called earlier, insisting he needed to talk to me. I told him I had to get to the church, but he pleaded with me. He said it couldn't wait."

An elderly couple holding hands walked by. They both smiled and said hello.

"Good evening." Molly acknowledged the two as they moved toward the water.

Derek cleared his throat. "I told my father I'd stop at the cleaners and would be over soon. I remember how my mind raced, wondering what in the world could be so urgent." He ran his foot over some loose pebbles.

"Do you want to walk some more? It might help."

Derek nodded and rose from the bench. They continued down the cement path, but this time, their hands remained at their sides.

"Cooked bacon. I'll never forget it. That's the first thing I smelled when I got to my parents' house and walked into the kitchen. I haven't eaten it again since that morning. I remember my mother and father were sitting at the table with plates of untouched food in front of them. The look on my mother's face—" Derek bit hard on his lower lip. He couldn't lose it now.

Molly reached for his hand. It gave him strength to continue.

"I thought my grandmother had died or some other relative. I remember how afraid I was to step closer to the table. Like there was some invisible line I'd cross and get sucked into whatever was going on. I didn't want to feel as bad as my parents looked at that moment."

"But you did," Molly stated.

"Yes. And it was worse than I ever could have imagined. My father had a relationship with a woman he worked with." Derek paused and forced a laugh. "She'd even been to our home for some social gatherings my parents hosted for my father's office."

Molly shook her head.

"At first, I thought the relationship had just started. But that wasn't the case. Before I had arrived at the house, my father had admitted to my mother he'd been having a relationship with her for over ten years."

Molly gasped at Derek's words.

"Yeah, well, it gets worse. He had children with her. Twin girls. I grew up thinking I was an only child, but in reality, I have two half sisters who are around eight years old now."

They reached the end of the sidewalk that ran parallel to the lake. Derek stopped and turned to face the water.

"I'm so sorry, Derek. I can't imagine learning something so shocking." Molly squeezed his hand.

"I've tried to forgive him, Molly. I have, but I can't move past the lie. For most of my life, I thought we had a perfect family. Sure, my father wasn't around much, but I still believed he loved me and my mother."

Molly glanced toward the stars. "I don't think there's such a thing as the perfect family."

Derek swallowed hard to push down the lump lodged in his throat. "I came to the same conclusion the day of your wedding. It's why I told Ryan he shouldn't get married."

Molly pulled her hand away and pressed it to her upper thigh.

"It was nothing against you. I tried to protect him. Or I thought I was. I wanted to make sure he knew there was no such thing as happily-ever-after. I told him what my father did was proof. Marriages don't last, and everyone involved gets their heart broken."

Molly held her silence for only a moment. "Don't you think that was something Ryan had the right to learn on his own?" She turned and started to head back in the direction they'd come from.

As she walked down the path, Derek considered her words. The moon cascaded across the back of Molly's shiny hair. He didn't move until she disappeared out of his sight, but her words remained. There might not be such a thing as a perfect family. A perfect man. Had he been wrong to believe his father was flawless, without defects? Just because his parents' marriage didn't work, did that have to mean all relationships were doomed? Perhaps it was time he realized that people made mistakes. On the day of Molly's wedding, he'd made one of his biggest mistakes ever by filling Ryan's head with doubt. It hadn't been his place. Looking back now, with a clear mind, Derek could see his error in judgment. He pivoted on his heel and headed up the trail.

Chapter Fourteen

Molly carried a yellow rocking chair from the corner of the children's area to the semicircle she'd formed around her seat.

"What time is Annie dropping off Grace?" Caitlin called out from behind the register where she'd been parked for the past hour, managing the social media accounts for the bookstore.

Molly was thrilled when she learned Caitlin, like Derek, was tech savvy. She knew all of the ins and outs when it came to the different platforms. The extra advertising had helped Molly see an uptick in sales this week. But would that, in combination with Mark's book signing tomorrow, be enough to save her store?

"She should be here within the hour. Thanks so much for agreeing to watch the store after Book Buddies. I need this alone time with Grace tonight."

Annie had called that morning to let her know she planned to drop off Grace for the book club tonight. Molly was excited but nervous about seeing the child. Their last time together at the picnic hadn't gone as she'd hoped. Much like her walk around the lake last night with Derek. She'd left him standing by the water's edge and hadn't seen him once today.

True, she'd felt terrible for him when he'd shared his family's secret, but it hadn't given him the right to ruin her future, as well. But had it really been all Derek's fault? Since their conversation at the lake, she couldn't help but wonder. Maybe Ryan had used Derek's news as a way to end their relationship. She couldn't ignore the fact that there had been a couple of times when Ryan suggested maybe they should wait a while longer before getting married. Had he felt pressured to propose marriage to her? If he'd truly loved her, would he have been able to walk away so easily? Would someone on the verge of committing their life to another person throw it all away with such ease?

She shuddered at the stab of pain and humiliation. Maybe no family was perfect, but that wouldn't stop her from having a family of her own.

"Sure, no problem," Caitlin said.

Molly needed to keep her mind off Derek.

She grabbed another chair and moved toward the register.

"I hope everything works out with the adoption, Molly. Grace seems like a sweet kid, and I know you'll make a wonderful mother."

Molly's heart danced at Caitlin's comment. The past few days, doubt had swarmed like gnats over a marsh. But it wasn't only her financial situation that left her questioning if she was qualified to be a mother. Was she being fair to Grace by adopting as a single mother? Didn't Grace deserve a complete family? Two parents. But then Molly thought of Shelley and how amazing she'd been at raising Molly as a single mom. "You think so?"

Caitlin looked up from the computer. "I know so."

An hour later, Molly's attention turned to the door as the overhead bell chimed and she heard the giggles of small children. She couldn't wait for time with Grace.

"Thanks for putting out the snacks, Caitlin. With all of that sugar, I hope the children will be able to sit still for the book reading." Molly watched as children swarmed the table loaded with treats. The school group attending this evening were second graders, but younger and a few older children also filled the store.

"You don't have to worry. You picked a great book for tonight."

This book held a special place in Molly's heart. It told the story of a girl who must decide which puppy to adopt from the animal shelter. As a child, she remembered reading it and feeling like the puppies. They'd wanted to be welcomed into a family and be loved. It had been her dream, too.

"Look, there's Grace," Caitlin announced.

Molly turned and spotted the child. She looked precious as ever dressed in blue jeans and a white sweater with little cherries on the front. Her honey-blond hair was pulled back with shiny barrettes on each side.

Annie and Grace moved toward the register. Molly watched as the child held tightly to Annie's hand while taking in her surroundings. When Grace looked in Molly's direction, a tiny smile parted the little girl's lips. A glimmer of hope ignited in Molly's heart. Could today be the day she made a connection?

"Hi, Molly. It looks like another good turnout for you." Annie smiled and leaned against the counter.

Molly noticed the crowd was larger than last week.

"Yes, it does. I'm glad you could come, Grace."

She looked down, smiled and brushed her hand over Grace's tiny shoulder.

"Is Mr. Derek coming tonight?"

Molly's heart sank. "I don't think so, but we'll have a good time. I promise."

Annie gave Molly a look of understanding and nodded. "I think you two will have a great time." She kneeled in front of Grace. "I'm going to head out. I'll be back to pick you up in a couple of hours."

Molly watched Grace. Would she refuse to stay behind? Thankfully, Grace nodded and looked toward Molly. "Can I go get a cookie?"

"Of course you can."

The grown-ups watched as Grace scurried toward the table of refreshments.

"Do you think I'm making progress with her? At least she's okay staying without you or Derek here."

Annie tugged on her purse strap. "Relax, she'll come around."

"I sure hope so."

"She was excited when I mentioned you want to take her to the Apple Harvest Festival. You'll have a great time," Annie said.

"So you're okay with me taking her?"

"Of course. I need to run. Have fun tonight." Annie turned and headed out the door.

Molly hoped Annie was right. It was one

thing to spend an hour or two with Grace, but an entire afternoon at the Apple Harvest Festival was different. The pressure would be on, but first Molly had to take advantage of the time she had this evening.

With Caitlin tending to the customers at the register, Molly seized the moment and approached with caution. She kept a close eye on Grace sitting at a table by a window that overlooked the courtyard. "That's always been one of my favorites." She commented on the book Grace had in front of her.

"Really? Mine, too." The child's face beamed like it had when she'd watched the video of Duke.

"Oh yes. Those children arc good detectives, don't you think?"

Grace reached for the book and studied the cover. Her nose crinkled. "I think it would be fun. They seem smart."

Molly slid into the empty chair. Grace appeared open to talk to her even though she didn't have a dog like Derek. Could books be a gateway into the child's heart? "Not all children like to read. I'm glad you seem to enjoy it."

Grace turned her gaze toward the window. "Sometimes I like to pretend I'm a character in the book."

Molly's chest tightened. Of course she did. "When I was your age, I did the same thing."

Her face brightened. "You did?"

Molly nodded. "Did Miss Annie tell you I was raised in foster care, too?" Molly had been nervous to address the subject, but the timing felt right.

"So your mommy didn't want you, either?"

Molly's ears burned. She'd asked herself the same question every day. It wasn't until she was older and adopted by Shelley that she understood her birth mother's reasons.

"When I was your age, I believed the same thing. But do you want to know something?"

Grace inched closer to Molly. "Yeah," she whispered.

"I always wondered who would adopt me when my own mother didn't even want me in her life."

"I think the same thing." Grace's back straightened.

Molly had been afraid of this. She wanted to take Grace into her arms and tell her she was wanted. That she was loved. But she had to be careful. Building Grace's trust was crucial. In Grace's eyes, Molly was another adult who couldn't be trusted.

"I know it's what you think, sweetie." She reached over for the child's hand.

Grace didn't pull away. She gazed down at their hands coupled as one and then a smile parted her lips.

A warmth like Molly had never felt traveled through her arm and straight to her heart. Was she finally having a breakthrough with Grace?

"Every time I go into a new foster home, the people act like they want me to be a part of their family. Then they turn out to be like my mommy and return me."

Molly's heart broke for the child. She'd been in Grace's shoes. A place no child deserved to be.

"Can I tell you something I learned?"

Grace shrugged.

"Once I got older, I realized my birth mother did love me."

Grace's brow crinkled. "How do you know? Did you see her again? Do you think I might see my mommy? I don't even know what she looks like."

"No, I never saw my mother, but the fact she chose to give me up for adoption is proof she did love me."

Grace's face was expressionless. "But how could throwing you away mean she loved you?"

"She didn't throw me away, sweetie. My mother wanted me to have a better life than she could provide. She was young and scared, and she realized adoption would give me more opportunities in life. And she was right."

Molly considered Grace. This was a lot to take in for someone her age, but the child appeared wise beyond her years.

"Did you end up with a good mommy?"

"The best. But it took a long time. Like you, I went from one home to another before I met my forever family." The similarities between her and Grace were chilling.

Grace placed her elbows on top of the table and rested her chin in the palms of her hands. "I get tired of moving. I want my own room with bookshelves filled with books and a dog like Duke."

"I want it for you, too, sweetie." She took in a deep breath. "I'd like to give you all of that and more, Grace."

Children's laughter carried through the store. The overhead light buzzed.

Grace focused her attention on the mother and daughter nibbling on cookies at the snack table. She looked back and met Molly's gaze. "Honest? You want to be my mommy?" Her tiny eyes flickered with hope.

Molly's eyes brimmed with tears. She'd never wanted something more in her life. "Yes, more than anything."

Grace stared at Molly as though she was

seeking truth in the adult eyes. During her short life, she probably hadn't encountered many truthful adults.

"Don't you want a baby? That's what everyone wants." The bell chimed over the front door, and Grace pivoted her head. "Mr. Derek!" She sprang from her chair and raced to him.

Molly's gut twisted. No. She wasn't ready for the conversation to be over. A wave of pain washed over her. She didn't want to adopt an infant. It was Grace who'd captured her heart from the moment she'd read her life story. God had brought Grace into her life for a purpose. *Oh, sweet baby girl, I'll give you the family you deserve. It might not be perfect, but you'll be loved. I promise.*

Derek tapped the backspace key on his laptop for the fifth time. After he'd picked up Mark from the airport and got him settled in the guest room, he'd been alone with his thoughts about his father and Molly. She'd avoided him the previous night when he'd come into the bookstore, but tomorrow that would be impossible.

Exhaling a long breath, he couldn't put it off any longer. He had to respond to his mother's email. Hunkered at the kitchen table, he rambled on about his new store. He explained how he'd been helping Molly and told her about his opportunity to purchase the space from Rusty. He also shared he wasn't able to get a large enough loan but had no plans to give up. Derek even wrote about Grace. How seeing her and Molly together was making him question his strong aversion to having a family, but he was still afraid to open his heart to the possibility of more pain. He'd left the hardest part—addressing her concerns about his relationship with his father—to last. She'd mentioned he was ill. How sick was he?

Footsteps sounded. The loose floorboard down the hall creaked.

Seconds later, Mark peeked his head into the room. "You're up late." The ice maker clunked, dropping cubes into the bin.

Derek pulled his eyes from the device. "I could say the same to you."

"No, I'm still on West Coast time."

"Right. Can I get you something?" Derek offered.

"I'm good. Thanks, though." Mark pulled out a chair and took a seat. "I guess being your own boss is a twenty-four-hour job."

"Actually, this is personal business. I'm writing to my mother." Derek explained the contents of his email. Mark was a good friend. He trusted him. Derek also shared how important it was to him to help Molly save her store.

"You could always ask your father to loan you the money," Mark suggested as he twirled a pen lying on the table.

After Derek had learned the truth about his father, he'd made the decision that he would never accept any financial help from him. "I'm not sure I could do that."

Mark nodded. "Not ready to forgive him yet?"

"It's complicated. I seem to waffle back and forth. I'm not sure I'll ever forget what he did."

"What about your mother? Didn't she move on?"

Learning his mother was dating had been a big adjustment, especially when she announced she was marrying her high school sweetheart. Derek had been speechless. "Yes, she has. She forgave my father and never looked back. She remarried five months ago."

"How do you feel about that?" Mark's eyebrows arched.

"At first, I struggled with it, but she's been through so much. All I want is for her to be happy. Of course, I'm keeping a close eye on this guy." Derek laughed. "Seriously, he's a great man, and he makes my mother happy. That's the important thing. I keep thinking, if she can move on, why can't I?" Derek had prayed for strength, but when it came to his father, he felt like a scared little boy.

"When was the last time you spoke with him?" Mark pushed away from the table and walked toward the refrigerator. "Do you want a bottle of water?"

At this moment, he could drink a gallon. Talking about his father sapped his energy. But was it making him feel better? "Sure. I haven't spoken to him since he sprang the news on me and my mother—over two years ago."

"It goes fast, doesn't it?" Mark passed him the water and took his seat.

Derek nodded. "It sure does. The sad thing is, I miss him."

"Why would you say it's sad?"

"Because look what he did. Not only to me, but to my mother. How could I miss someone who ripped my family apart?"

"Look, Derek. I won't pretend to be an expert on the subject, but you need to let this go. I never made peace with my father, and now it's too late."

Derek remembered going to the funeral for Mark's father. The man had been diagnosed with cancer, and three months later, he was gone. Derek was aware Mark had had a strained relationship with his father, but he didn't know the details. "I'm sorry."

"Thanks. Listen, buddy, I'm not trying to tell you what to do. I'm giving you fair warning. If you don't make peace with your father, it will eat you alive. I'm living proof. I would give anything for the opportunity to tell my father I forgive him—to sit down and talk. It's too late for me." Mark took a long swig from his bottle of water. "Don't let it pass for you, too. I'm going to hit the hay. Let's hope for a big day tomorrow." Mark rose from the table and patted his friend's shoulder.

"Let's hope so. Good night, bud." Derek traced his finger down the side of his water bottle.

An hour after Mark had gone to bed, Derek still sat in his dark kitchen. The house was quiet except for the hum of the refrigerator. Outside the window, a barred owl screeched, making his presence known. With the glow of the blue light from his laptop, Derek poured his thoughts, anger, fears and hopes into an email to his father. He apologized for expecting perfection from his father. He spoke of his feelings for Molly, and how he still struggled with the belief that relationships weren't worth the risk of heartache.

After an hour of nonstop typing, he stared at his words while his finger hovered over the send button. Every feeling he'd experienced since learning the truth was documented. His hand shook when it moved toward the delete button. No. Mark was right. He had to make peace. Not to make his father feel better, but for himself. Forgiveness was the only way he could move on with his life. How could he ask for Molly's forgiveness when he wasn't capable of giving the gift himself? With one stroke of a key, Derek's shoulders relaxed as the email was in transit to his father.

The following afternoon, Derek sucked in a deep breath before opening the door to Bound to Please Reads. He and Molly hadn't cleared the air following their discussion at the lake on Tuesday evening. When he'd popped into the store before Book Buddies on Wednesday to drop off some marketing information for the presentation Caitlin planned to do for her class next week, Molly had hurried off to assist a customer, but the look she'd thrown his way had told him she wasn't open for conversation. It was just as well. The shop was busy, so it wouldn't have been a good time to talk. He'd said a quick hi to Grace and left.

Today, they couldn't avoid each other. Mark would be at the store any minute to set up for his book signing. This day was all about saving Molly's store. It wasn't the time to discuss their past.

Whoa. Derek stopped and had to remind himself to breathe when he spotted Molly assisting a middle-aged man scanning books in the health section. Her hair was swept away from her face in a loose ponytail that highlighted her high cheekbones. She looked stunning. Dressed in a fitted black pantsuit, a white blouse and high-heeled shoes, she meant business.

Molly glanced in his direction, and he lifted his hand to give a quick wave. Her lips barely parted into a smile. If he had blinked, he would have missed it. Yep. She might understand the pain he endured the morning of the wedding after learning the truth about his father, but she definitely didn't understand why he had to drag her and Ryan into his messy life. He couldn't understand it then, but he did now, and he'd been wrong.

"Hey, bud."

Derek turned as Mark crossed through the front entrance carrying a silver tumbler. "You're early."

"Yeah, my agent called. A courier is scheduled to deliver the books, along with some freebies. I didn't want Molly to be bothered with it. Plus, I wanted to have time to meet her and thank her for hosting me."

A truck rumbled outside. "That's my delivery." Mark placed his beverage on a nearby table.

"After I give you a hand, I'll introduce you to Molly." Derek peered over his shoulder, but she was no longer helping the customer or at the register. He'd check her office after he helped Mark.

Fifteen minutes later, the boxes of books were stacked against the wall adjoining the children's section. Molly had mentioned the area would be the best place for Mark's signing table. She'd already set out a pitcher of water along with a glass and several pens. He scanned the store. "I saw Molly earlier— Oh, here she comes."

Molly crossed the store from her office, straightening her jacket. "I am so sorry. I got caught on the phone with an out-of-town customer who plans to visit this weekend."

Derek smiled. The website was working. This was good news. "Molly, this is Mark Potter. Mark, Molly." He gestured his hand between the two.

"It's a pleasure to meet you, Molly. I wanted to say thanks for hosting me at your lovely shop."

Molly's cheeks reddened. "Oh, trust me, the pleasure is all mine. I'm a huge fan of your books."

"I appreciate it. Derek tells me you're a writer, too." Mark bent over, reached for a box of his books and placed it on the table.

Molly glanced in Derek's direction before turning back to Mark. "I've sold a few short stories, but nothing like what you've accomplished."

"That's wonderful. Can I give you one piece of advice to carry along in your writer's toolbox?"

Molly clasped her hands together. "Oh yes, please."

"Don't ever compare yourself to others. This is your journey, and yours alone. Comparing it with others' will steal your joy quicker than anything."

Molly nodded. "I'll remember that. Thank you."

"Derek mentioned you're working on a novel. If you ever need a reader, I'd be happy to take a look at it," Mark offered.

Derek laughed when Molly's eyes practically popped out of her head.

"Oh my," she squealed. "I wouldn't want to take up your time. I know how busy successful writers can be."

"Trust me, I get tired of reading my stuff all of the time. My email is on my website. Feel free to contact me anytime." Mark turned to the front door.

Derek laughed as the man delivering the books carried in a life-size cardboard photograph of Mark holding a copy of his latest release. "What in the world?"

"Come on, man. Don't laugh. My publisher likes to have this on display when I do a signing. It wasn't my idea." Mark shook his head.

Molly jumped like an excited child and clapped her hands. "Oh, how wonderful. We'll put it at the front entrance so people can see it as they pass by." She hurried off to set up the display.

"We don't want to scare off the customers," Derek joked and fist-bumped Mark's arm.

"Thanks, buddy."

Derek bent down and retrieved the last of the books. "You know I'm kidding. I appreciate what you're doing here. Saving this store is important to Molly."

"Just Molly?" Mark's eyes widened. "Is there something going on with you and her?"

Across the room, Molly fiddled with the display. She looked over and smiled, igniting Derek's senses. He turned to answer Mark's question, but a part of him feared to admit his feelings. He was afraid to trust his heart to another person like he'd trusted his father. "No. I'm looking out for my business."

Chapter Fifteen

Molly tried to keep her eyes off Derek and on the task at hand. Rescuing her store. That's what this night was about. The place was mobbed with excited readers anxious to snag a copy of Mark Potter's latest release, and for a chance to meet the author. Derek's idea was nothing short of genius. Molly and Caitlin struggled to keep pace with the customers making purchases to get a free autographed copy of Mark's book.

"I've never seen the store this crowded," Caitlin exclaimed. "I think people are coming from all over the state of Virginia."

Molly agreed. There had been some local townspeople who'd rallied to show support for Molly's store, but the majority of the faces were unfamiliar.

Molly sent up a silent prayer that the sales from this evening's event would be enough to pay Rusty what she owed him in rent. Then what? How would she get back on track and start saving money? Annie had told her not to worry about her financial situation impacting her ability to adopt Grace, but how could it not? No one was going to give a child to someone who couldn't support her.

"Hey, are you okay, Molly?" Caitlin rested her hand on Molly's back.

She bit her lower lip and shook her head. "I'm fine." But she knew she wasn't. "Can you cover the register?" Molly rounded the counter.

"Sure, no problem."

She was two steps short from making it inside her office when the tears erupted. She closed the door but couldn't escape the thoughts consuming her mind. *You still could lose everything. The store. Your home. And most importantly of all—Grace.*

Moments passed before a soft knock sounded at the door. Molly snatched a tissue from the box on her desk and blotted her eyes.

"Molly. Can I come in?"

Derek.

She couldn't face him. Not now. "I'll be out in a minute."

The door squeaked as Derek slowly pushed it open.

Molly turned to see his head peeking inside.

"Caitlin said you were upset. Do you want to talk about it?"

He approached with caution. "Hey, what's with the tears? Tonight is supposed to be a good night for you and your store. Things are going great out there."

Derek pulled another tissue from the box and stepped closer. He wiped away the tears racing down her cheek.

"I know. I'm so sorry." She took a deep breath and closed her eyes. "You've done so much. And Mark coming here— You've both been so generous, but—"

"What? Why are you so upset? Please, talk to me, Mols."

She wasn't sure if it was the sincerity in his smoldering eyes or the masculine scent of his aftershave, but she couldn't clear her mind enough to explain her actions.

"You can trust me. I know you think you can't because of what I did to you in the past, but you can."

"I feel like I've been treading water the past few weeks. I don't think I can keep going. What if tonight isn't enough to bring me out of debt?"

"Haven't you noticed the crowd out there? Molly, there's a line outside the door that goes clear down the sidewalk."

The last thing she wanted to do was sound

ungrateful, but she had to be realistic. "I know there's a lot of people. And maybe I'll make enough to pay Rusty. But what happens next? The end of this month is coming up, so another rent payment is almost due. Even if you're able to buy the place from Rusty, you can't allow me to stay if I'm unable to pay you rent." She stepped back and wrapped her arms tightly across her stomach. "Don't you get it? I'm a failure. I'll never be able to get ahead. My dream of family is over."

Derek moved in closer and placed his hand underneath her chin, tipping her head to him. Their eyes locked. "You will have everything you've ever dreamed of having. I promise."

Molly felt a force pulling her closer to Derek, but he wasn't moving. It was her. She was leaning toward him, unable to put on the brakes. She felt his breath as she fell into his arms. He buried his nose in her hair.

"You'll have that family, Molly." He shifted his head so they were face-to-face. "I promise."

Molly leaned closer, and with a slight movement, Derek closed the space between them. Their lips brushed, and she melted deeper into his muscular build, longing to stay there forever.

"Molly." Caitlin stepped through the open office door and froze. "Oh, I'm sorry."

Molly jumped, and Derek moved away quickly, but for a moment, she yearned to be back in his arms and wished the kiss had lasted longer.

"What's wrong, Caitlin?" Molly ran her hands through her hair.

"Annie's out front. She said she needs to speak with you." Caitlin scurried out of the room, obviously embarrassed by the interruption.

Molly's mind swirled. Had Annie come to meet Mark, or was she here to deliver news Molly wasn't ready to hear?

Derek moved closer. "Are you okay?"

"I don't have a good feeling. It's probably bad news. I know it is. I'm going to lose Grace."

"Relax. Maybe she's here to support you. Go and talk to her. I'm sure it's nothing."

Molly had missed a call from Annie earlier in the day, but with the excitement swirling about this evening's event, she'd forgotten about it.

"Molly? Do you need me to go with you?"

A desire to be back in his arms consumed her. When Derek had taken her into his comforting embrace, she'd felt safe for the first time in years. She realized in the last several weeks that she'd grown to need him more than she wanted to admit to herself. "Do you mind?"

Derek placed his hand on the small of her back and a shiver traveled down her spine. "Of course not. Let's go."

Outside the office, Molly's eyes canvassed the store. The crowd had expanded.

"Wow," Derek exclaimed. "I hope the fire marshal doesn't shut the place down."

Molly's jaw tightened. "They wouldn't do that, would they?"

"Relax. I'm joking. Look, there's Annie over there talking to Mrs. Buser." Derek pointed toward the group of chairs closest to the front door.

Molly forced down the lump that had lodged in her throat when Caitlin announced Annie's visit. She sent up a silent prayer. More than ever, she needed to trust God and His timing. If it wasn't the time for her to bring a child into her life, she'd have to accept it. But how? She'd fallen in love with Grace. Molly's stomach turned over at the thought of Grace in someone else's home, especially if the home was anything like those she'd experienced so far.

Auntie Elsie spoke first. "Well, hello, dear. You should be thrilled with the turnout tonight."

It was a dream come true. Under different circumstances, Molly would be over the moon, but she knew one successful night might not be enough. Of course, that wasn't fair to Derek, or to Mark. "Oh yes, I am. I couldn't ask for more. It's been a terrific evening so far."

"I've purchased a book on Ireland, so I'm going to go get in line." Elsie reached out and squeezed Molly's hand. "We'll chat later." The elderly woman went out the door to claim her spot in the line snaking down the sidewalk.

Molly turned to Annie. "Are you here for a copy of Mark's book, too?" *Please let that be the reason.*

Annie tucked a strand of her hair behind her ear. "Yes, I love his books."

Molly's shoulders relaxed. She wouldn't lose Grace. At least not today.

"But I also hoped we could talk. I know you're busy, but it's important."

Why hadn't she answered Annie's call? She'd delayed the inevitable. "I'm sorry I didn't respond to you earlier. It's been a chaotic day."

"Do you want to go somewhere and talk in private?" Annie glanced at Derek before looking back to Molly.

What was the point? Derek already knew how her financial struggles could impact the adoption procedure. "That won't be necessary. Derek is familiar with my situation. Let's just step over there." Molly pointed to a quiet corner of the store and braced herself for whatever Annie had to say.

"I was wrong to tell you not to be concerned about your financial situation, Molly. I wish I'd never said it."

"What is it, Annie? Am I going to lose Grace?"

Molly flinched when Derek took her hand, but it gave her the strength she needed. "Please, tell me."

"All hope isn't lost. I just wanted to let you know your file has been flagged for further review of your finances."

The chatter of excited readers went silent. A muffled tone filled Molly's ears, reminding her of when she'd been knocked over by a large wave during her first trip to the ocean with Shelley. Tossed about in the swift current, unsure of which direction would bring her to the surface, Molly hadn't been able to get her bearings. After it happened, she'd never gotten back into the surf again. Playing in the sand was where she'd spent the remainder of the trip. She drew in a breath and exhaled. This was understandable. The agency had to look after Grace's best interests. She couldn't fault them. "Okay. So what happens next?"

Annie fingered the gold locket around her neck. "I suppose we'll have to wait and see what they determine. Try not to get discouraged. Keep doing what you're doing. I'll drop Grace off at your house around ten o'clock tomorrow morning, if that works for you?"

"That's perfect," Molly answered. At least she had something to look forward to. She couldn't think of anything she'd rather do than spend the day with Grace. Just the two of them. She couldn't allow Annie's news tonight to spoil the excitement. She had to continue to cling to her faith and believe in the impossible—in promises.

"She's looking forward to the festival."

A lightness filled Molly's chest. "She is? Did she say something about it?"

"Yes. She's excited about the animals at the petting zoo."

Molly had hoped the excitement was stirred by the idea of spending time with her, but she couldn't blame Grace. "Those baby goats are adorable."

"I better get going. Wishing you the best tonight, guys. I'll see you in the morning, Molly." She whirled around and headed out the door.

"You okay?" Derek asked, moving in closer. "Relax, you and Grace will have a great time tomorrow."

Molly nodded. "I'm okay." But it wasn't true. She wasn't sure she'd ever recover if she lost her bookstore and Grace in one swoop.

Two hours later, the crowd had thinned and Mark had signed the last book. He stood from the table and shook out his hand. "Wow, I don't think I've ever signed so many books in one night."

Molly stepped closer. "Thank you so much for coming tonight, Mark. It meant the world to me."

"I'll come back anytime, Molly. I hope things work out for you. You have a wonderful store. It would be a shame for you to close."

The thought made Molly queasy. "Thank you, Mark. I've been doing a lot of thinking about what I would do if I have to close my store. I'm not sure I could stay in Whispering Slopes. There would be nothing left for me here except too many sad memories."

"Move? But this is your home." Derek's brow crinkled.

"If I lose the bookstore and my chance at adopting Grace, there's no reason for me to stay. The best thing I could do is start over in a new city." These thoughts had raced through her mind at all hours of the night.

Molly felt Derek's eyes burning into the side of her face. Was it that big a surprise to hear she'd want to leave Whispering Slopes if her business failed? Did he think the kiss they'd shared earlier meant anything? The kiss should never have happened. And after tonight, she'd make sure there wasn't a repeat performance. Derek McKinney had already caused enough heartbreak in her life.

Molly plans to leave town? This was news to him. An hour later, Derek remained numb after Molly's shocking announcement. She loved Whispering Slopes, and the people in this town loved her. He couldn't let that happen. As much as he'd tried to fight it, he was falling in love with her. Was he ready to accept the risks involved in opening his heart to the possibility of a relationship with Molly?

"Well, it looks like I'm about ready to go." Mark zipped his leather satchel and flung the strap over his shoulder.

Derek rounded the counter. "Don't you want to wait and find out what the final tally is from tonight?"

Mark shook his head. "The way my hand feels, I think Molly's sales broke an all-time record." He made a fist. "I'm finally getting the feeling back in my fingers. I need to get back to your house and soak my hands in some Epsom salts." He laughed and extended his arm over the counter to Molly. "I hope it all works out for you. But whatever you do, keep writing. And remember my offer still stands to read your work."

Molly shook his hand and smiled. "Thank you for everything, Mark. I appreciate it. Who knows? If things work out, maybe you can come back when your next book is released."

Derek considered the tone of Molly's comment. She doubted she'd ever see Mark or host another signing again. When the front door closed behind his friend, Derek turned to her. "Are you ready to do some calculating? I have a good feeling about this." He smiled in an attempt to lighten the mood.

Following an hour and a half of tabulations behind the register, the numbers didn't lie.

"Do you want me to count it one more time?" Derek hoped counting for a third time would change the bottom line, but he knew it wouldn't. The sales were good, but not good enough to cover both this month's rent and the next as well as the money she owed to vendors. This event had been a long shot, and Derek truly believed it had gone well for Molly. It would buy her more time with Rusty.

Molly shook her head. "There's no point, Derek." Her tone remained defeated.

No. He wouldn't allow Molly to surrender her dream of owning a successful store and bringing Grace into her home.

Derek's heart squeezed when Molly covered her face to hide the tears trickling down her cheeks. "Please, don't cry. We'll figure this out. Whatever you do, don't make any rash decisions."

"I have to do something, Derek. Once my store closes, I can't stay here and watch Grace go and live with another family. It's too painful. And I won't continue to lead Grace on and fill her with false hope. I'll have to tell her tomorrow." Molly snatched a tissue from a box behind the counter and wiped away the tears. "It could be time for a new start. There are too many memories here in Whispering Slopes."

Silence hung in the air.

Molly tossed the tissue into the trash can. "I think it's time to call it a night. I'm exhausted, and you need to get home to Mark. Thank you again for everything you've done. I know you've tried your best, but I guess some things aren't meant to be."

Molly turned and headed to her office, leaving Derek alone and feeling desperate. He had to fix this. But how? She couldn't move. Whispering Slopes was her home. She belonged here. And he belonged here, too—with Molly and Grace.

It was time he started to trust God and move

past his fears. It was okay to be vulnerable. He didn't need a promise from Molly that she'd never hurt him. That a life with her would be perfect and free of problems. No. That was unrealistic. It was time to take risks again, like he'd always done in business. Vulnerability was a strength, not a weakness. Could Molly and Grace be the family he'd once dreamed of having? Derek considered his thoughts and smiled. He'd never had a dream he couldn't turn into a reality.

Later in the evening, Derek sat in his home office slumped over his laptop, replaying the events from earlier. His computer chimed, announcing a new email. Mindlessly, he slid his finger over the mouse. His adrenaline raced when he saw the subject line next to his father's email address. I can help you. Those words sent Derek's mind reeling. Could his father help? Could the man who'd caused him to second-guess everything he'd once believed help him to discover there was such a thing as happily-ever-after?

Minutes passed. He stared at the screen, feeling like that frightened little boy who used to bury his head in the pillow when he heard sirens outside his window at night. His hand shook. He opened the email, and began to read his father's three-page apology and a request for forgiveness. At the end, there was an offer to help his only son.

Chapter Sixteen

Before dawn on Saturday morning, Molly paced the floor in her kitchen. The coffee maker gurgled and hissed. The aroma of the fresh brew filled the room. She'd been awake for an hour reading her Bible and praying for guidance. As a child, countless times she'd been hopeful and believed a family wanted to adopt her, only to be left brokenhearted and disappointed. She couldn't do that to Grace. Today at the festival, she'd have to be honest with her. As much as she wanted to bring Grace into her home, it might not be possible. The thought of such a discussion filled Molly's heart with sadness.

Later, after a long walk to clear her head, Molly was dressed and waiting for Annie's arrival. Her pulse accelerated when she heard car doors slam outside. Footsteps clomped on the front steps. The doorbell rang, and Molly exhaled. Until last night, she'd been so excited about this day and looking forward to spending time alone with Grace, but now, dread had taken hold.

Molly crossed the floor and made her way toward the door. While taking those steps, she decided if today would be the last time she'd have with Grace, she would make sure the child had the best day ever. She placed her hand on the doorknob to welcome her company.

"Good morning, Molly. I'm running late as usual." Annie smiled, handed the car seat to Molly and looked down at Grace. "You have a good time today with Miss Molly. You can tell me all about your day when I come to get you this evening. Have fun, you two."

"Thanks, Annie," Molly called out as the social worker turned and headed to her car. "Are you ready to have some big fun?" Molly motioned for Grace to come inside.

The child stepped into the foyer and looked in Molly's direction. "I can't wait!" Grace's dimples flashed like a shining ray of hope.

Molly's heart filled with joy. Grace would have the best day of her life. Molly had a feeling it was going to be an extra special day.

Fifteen minutes into their drive, Molly snuck a glance at Grace in the rearview mirror as she navigated the car along the mountain road. Her heart pulsed as she imagined going on daily outings as mother and daughter. Spending an afternoon shopping for back-to-school clothes or picking out a wedding dress after Grace fell in love. In a matter of weeks, this child had filled a void, one Molly had tried to ignore because she believed having a family was an impossible dream after she'd been left at the altar. Lately, the yearning for a family was palpable. Molly longed to give Grace the home she'd dreamed of when she was a child.

"Did you ever go to this festival when you were my age, Miss Molly?" Secured in the car seat Annie had provided, Grace leaned forward, squinting into the sun streaming through the front windshield.

"I didn't move to Whispering Slopes until I was a teenager. That's when I was adopted. After that, my mother brought me to the festival every year."

A sigh sounded from the back seat. Molly stole brief glances in the mirror.

"Are you okay, sweetie?" Molly considered the fret in Grace's brows.

"I'm sorry you had to wait so long, Miss Molly. If I hadn't met you, I probably would—" She inhaled through her nostrils.

"What's wrong?"

"Nothing. It's just, I shouldn't get my hopes up. None of the other families ever wanted me around." She peered out the window. "I think most people take me in for the money."

Molly's heart broke. Grace was living the life she'd experienced. Ahead, Molly spotted the first overlook area where Shelley had brought her. It was there Molly had learned of Shelley's plan to make a permanent home for her. Molly guided the vehicle off the road to where several empty picnic tables stood. "Let's pull over for a second."

Molly placed the car in Park. She stepped out, opened Grace's door and unlocked her seat belt. Grace climbed out onto the gravel parking lot and turned her attention to the four-foot-high stone wall providing safety to spectators.

The child's head jerked back at Molly. "Wow! You can see forever up here."

They strolled toward the wall. Molly's pulse quickened at the soft touch of Grace's hand reaching for her own. Molly wanted to hold it tightly forever.

Grace stood on her tippy-toes and looked down with a firm grip on Molly's hand. "I've never been this high. Everything looks so clear and bright. Do you think this is what heaven is like, Miss Molly?"

Molly could only nod. Her throat tightened.

She'd asked her mother the same question. Forcing down the lump caught in her throat, she gazed at the spectacular skyline. "I'd like to think so, sweetie. Let's go and sit over there for a minute." She pointed to the picnic table that still provided a view.

Grace kept a secure grip on Molly's hand but skipped along by her side. "I like it here."

Molly laughed. The child's enthusiasm was contagious. Grace released her hold and plopped down on the bench, squirming to ensure she still had a view. Molly settled in across from her.

"My mother brought me here to tell me she loved me and wanted to adopt me." Molly gazed at the area. The leaves popped with color, and the air was crisp. "It was a day like today."

"What did it feel like?"

Molly locked her eyes on the little girl. "You mean the weather?"

Grace wiggled, her jeans scratching against the wooden seat. "No. What did it feel like when you heard someone say they loved you?"

Molly's heart crumbled. Her vision blurred as she wiped a tear. "Oh, sweetie. You are loved. You must always remember God loves you. He loved you first. He'll never leave you."

Grace looked at the crow cawing overhead. Her brow crinkled. "But how come God isn't listening to my prayers?"

Given the homes Grace had been in and out of, Molly was surprised to learn Grace was aware of the power of prayer. "Who taught you about praying, sweetie?"

"Mrs. Mayfield. She was a nice, white-haired lady who lived next door to one of the homes I lived in, but I was only there for two weeks. I missed her when I had to leave."

"Why such a short time?" Molly questioned with caution, worried she would spark any painful memories.

Grace's expression grew more solemn. Not what Molly wanted today. She reached for the child's hand and covered it with her own. "You don't have to talk about it if you don't want to."

Grace sat straighter. "The social worker came and removed me from the house." Her lower lip quivered. "The lady I lived with burned me with hot water from the bathtub."

Bile burned in the back of her throat. "Oh dear. Could it have been an accident?"

Grace shook her head. "No. Whenever she drank a lot of bad stuff, she got mean. One day, Mrs. Mayfield found me crying outside after the lady had held my arm under the water for a really long time. Mrs. Mayfield told me to pray for a new home."

Molly recalled the picnic. That's why Grace had been afraid of the river.

A second of silence passed before Grace looked at Molly. "Do you think I'll have to wait until I'm a teenager before God answers my prayers?"

Molly would do everything in her power to make sure that didn't happen. "It's important for us to place our trust in God's timing."

"Yeah, that's what Mrs. Mayfield used to say." Grace put her elbows on the table and palmed her chin. "But I sure wish His clock moved faster."

Molly laughed out loud. "So do I, sweetie. So do I."

Following an afternoon of pony and hay rides, Molly couldn't remember a time when she'd been this happy. She and Grace strolled the grounds of the festival, each munching on a caramel apple. "I forgot how these stick to your teeth." Molly flicked her tongue along an upper molar.

"It's what makes them so good." Grace giggled. "Oh look! It's the petting zoo. Can we go there next? I can't wait to see the baby goats." The child bounced up and down, her pigtails swinging.

"Of course. I've been excited to see them, too." Molly and Grace headed toward the fenced area. Leaves crunched underneath their feet. "When I was your age, I always wanted a baby goat and a monkey," Molly revealed.

"Me, too! If I had a monkey, I'd name it George." Grace smiled.

"Like the book?"

Grace nodded. "Yeah, it's one of my favorites."

"Mine, too," Molly added, and Grace reached for her hand.

Children's laughter carried on a soft breeze when they arrived at the fencing. A half-dozen kids were romping on the ground, playing with the goats.

Grace stopped. "You're going to come in, too, aren't you?"

One look into the child's sparkling eyes, and she was a goner. Molly took the remainder of Grace's apple and along with her own, tossed them both into a nearby trash can. "Are you kidding? I wouldn't miss it for the world."

A cupcake-for-breakfast grin crossed the child's face. Her deep-set dimples shined as they stepped inside of the corral.

Within seconds, a black-and-white goat, the smallest of the group, ran toward Grace. She flopped to the ground and laughed as the animal bounded into her lap. "He likes me, Miss Molly!"

"It sure seems like it," Molly called out as a

solid chestnut goat headed her way. She dropped to the grass, and the animal butted its head against her arm.

Giggling, Grace looked in her direction. "I think that one likes you."

After forty-five minutes of frolicking with the baby goats, Molly's stomach grumbled. "Are you ready for a slice of pizza?"

"Yes! Yes! That's my favorite!"

"Mine, too."

"We like a lot of the same things, don't we, Miss Molly?" The child grinned.

"I think you're right. Let's head to the restroom and wash our hands before we eat." Molly gulped a breath. She knew explaining to Grace her current financial situation and its impact on the adoption process was necessary. But how could she disappoint her? She was having so much fun. *Please, Lord, give me the words.*

Ten minutes later, Molly and Grace ate their lunch in the area that resembled a food court at the mall. "This is the best pizza ever," Grace exclaimed. A string of cheese stretched before snapping and getting stuck to her chin. She giggled and used her tongue to lick it off. "You're the best, Miss Molly! I wish you could be my mommy."

Molly's breath hitched. This was the day she'd dreamed of having with Grace. Not only was the weather perfect for the festival, but this time with Grace had been the perfect balm. Was she being selfish? Would Grace's heart be broken like hers had been at her age? She still remembered how painful it was when her chance to be adopted by the Corbett family had been stripped away. Withholding the truth would be worse for Grace in the long run. As much as she didn't want to see this glorious day come to an end, it was time to be honest. No matter how painful, she couldn't continue to mislead Grace.

Derek couldn't contain the excitement surging through his body. Earlier that morning, his father had called after receiving the second email from his son. Following an hour of angry words spoken by Derek, and a lot of tears shed, father and son had made peace with the past and agreed to start fresh. Derek had let go of the judgment and grievances, not just for his father's sake, but for his own. It was the only way to begin the healing process and move on with his life. A life he wanted to spend with Molly. He loved her. The kiss they'd shared told him she felt the same, yet she'd convinced herself leaving Whispering Slopes was the best solution. Well, it wasn't. If she wanted a new start, a new life, he planned to offer it to her. Today, while she was still at the festival with Grace.

He white-knuckled the steering wheel and guided the vehicle into the parking lot. He exhaled a steadying breath when he spotted Rusty stepping inside the coffee shop. After speaking with his father, Derek had made a phone call and asked his landlord to meet him.

Seconds later, Derek zipped into an empty space and smashed his foot on the brake. He was on a mission. Molly had mentioned her plans to talk to Grace today about how much she wanted to make a home for her, but financial obstacles were standing in the way. He couldn't let that happen. Grace would be crushed. He loved the child as much as Molly. He exited the car and jogged to the front entrance of the store.

"Hey, Derek." Rusty stood at the counter. "What's got you so charged today, son?"

Derek ran his hand through his hair. "Can we talk over there?" He pointed to an empty table in the corner. "Coffee?"

"No thanks. Let's take a seat."

Derek's adrenaline surged. He couldn't sit still long enough to string two sentences together. When he finally settled down, his heart opened, and the words flowed. He told Rusty everything—about his father and his feelings for Molly. Fifteen minutes later, in the quiet corner of his coffee shop, Derek and Rusty sealed the deal on the property with a handshake.

"I have to say, son, when you want something, you go after it." Rusty smiled, energized by the news.

"I couldn't have done any of this if it weren't for my father. For the past two years, I couldn't accept that my father had flaws. I allowed his actions to alter what I wanted for my life."

"None of us are without flaws, son."

Derek nodded. "It took time for me to come to that realization. I'm thankful my father and I have been able to put what happened in the past behind us and start over. I hope Molly can do the same. I know she means the world to you. I love her, too, and I want to spend the rest of my life making her happy."

Rusty reached across the table and gripped Derek's hand. "From the first time I saw the two of you together, I knew your lives were meant to become one. You have my blessing, son."

"Thank you, sir." The two men said their goodbyes, and once outside the coffee shop, Derek slipped his phone from his pocket. He had one more person he needed to speak with before heading to the festival to find Molly.

Fifteen minutes later, Derek pulled into the gravel parking lot. Children's laughter and music swirled in the air. The sweet aroma of kettle corn tempted his taste buds. He exhaled a deep breath when he spotted Annie standing near the pumpkin carving station. He moved toward her.

"I'm so excited for the three of you." Annie squeezed Derek's forearm. "Thank you for calling me. They're over by the fountain." Annie nodded toward the Ferris wheel and gave him two thumbs up.

Derek sprinted across the grassy field to the cement patio where the fountain sat surrounded by park benches. He hoped Molly hadn't talked with Grace about the adoption yet. His heart squeezed when he spotted them each tossing a coin into the water.

"Mr. Derek!" Grace's eyes popped wide open, and she ran toward him.

"Hey, kiddo!" He scooped her into his arms and spun her around.

Grace giggled. "I can't believe you're here! I hoped for that before I threw my penny into the water."

Molly approached Derek. Her brow crinkled. "What are you doing here?"

Next, she turned to face Annie, who had moved toward them. "Annie? I thought you were going to pick up Grace at my house tonight."

Derek kneeled so he was face-to-face with Grace. "Sweetie, you go with Miss Annie for a minute while I speak with Miss Molly."

"But I don't want to go." The child's lip quivered. "I want to stay with you guys."

"Grace, come along." Annie motioned for the child.

Grace's shoulders slumped as she trudged toward the social worker.

Molly faced Derek, and her floral scent drifted toward him.

"Why is Grace leaving with Annie? I haven't had a chance to talk to her about the adoption. I have to be the one to tell her that I can't be her mommy."

The moment Derek saw the tears starting to stream down Molly's cheeks, he stepped closer and took her into his arms. Rubbing his hand on the back of her head, he whispered into her ear. "You can be her mommy. You can have everything you've ever dreamed of."

Molly slowly pulled her head back but remained in his arms. "I don't understand. What are you talking about?"

Derek's heart pounded against his chest. "I

love you, Molly." He paused, searching for the right words so she would understand his motives. "You and Grace have brought a sense of meaning and purpose back into my life. I'd allowed my father's actions to control my future. I'm not going to use that as an excuse any longer. I want to make a happy life for you and Grace. It might not be perfect, but I promise you I'll do the best I can."

Molly remain silent, obviously trying to digest what he had revealed.

"Are you okay?"

She focused her eyes on him. "You love me? But I thought you didn't like me."

Derek laughed. "Oh, I more than like you." He dropped to the ground, kneeled on one knee and placed his hands around hers. "I want to spend the rest of my life with you and Grace. We can adopt her as a married couple and be her forever family."

"But…my store. I can't stay in Whispering Slopes and watch it be turned into office space."

"That's not going to happen. My father and I talked early this morning."

Molly smiled. "I'm happy to hear that, but I don't understand what that has to do with my shop."

"I had to let it go. The anger I've held on to for so long. It was wrong, especially since I

want to move on and share my life with someone. With you. God is so good. He gave me the
grace I needed to forgive my father for what
he did to my family. My father wants to lend
us the money to purchase the property. I've already spoken with Rusty."

Derek stood, still holding Molly's hands.
"So, what do you say?"

"First, I need to say I'm sorry. You had a
good reason to go to Ryan the day of our wedding. You were hurt and confused. I shouldn't
have put all of the blame on you. Ryan didn't
have to react to what you told him. He made
a choice, and that choice wasn't me. I didn't
see it then, but now I know it was for the best.
I would never have met Grace if Ryan hadn't
dumped me. And I would never have had the
chance to fall in love with you."

"So, does that mean you think you could
marry me?"

Molly placed her hand on the side of his face.
"Well, I guess it all depends."

Derek's stomach twisted. Was she going to
turn him down? He couldn't imagine his life
without her. "On what?"

"Do you think you could learn to like mushrooms on your pizza?" A devious smile parted
her lips.

Derek took her into his arms. "Most definitely!"

The couple laughed and shared a kiss before Derek pulled away. "What do you say we go get our daughter and take a ride on the Ferris wheel?"

Epilogue

"Close your eyes," Derek instructed Molly.

Grace squealed with delight. Jumping up and down, she clapped her hands while holding Duke's leash.

Molly's heart raced. "But you've kept this a secret long enough. I can't stand it any longer."

"Good things come to those who wait, Mrs. McKinney," Derek whispered into his bride's ear.

Chills traveled through her body. *Mrs. McKinney.* After Derek had confessed his love and proposed to her at the festival, the months that followed had been a whirlwind, starting with an intimate wedding on Christmas Eve. After the holidays, they had finalized the adoption of Grace and welcomed her home. She had legally become their daughter. Molly's dreams had come true thanks to her gorgeous husband.

"Okay, watch your step." He placed his hand on the small of her back, guiding her inside.

Molly smelled a combination of fresh paint and coffee. What in the world? She never served coffee in her bookstore. After Derek proposed, he'd told Molly once they were married, he wanted to close her store for a few weeks. He didn't provide any details other than that it was his wedding gift to her. She'd still operated her online business, but in-store sales and all of the bookstore activities had been put on hold. And under no circumstances had she been allowed to come anywhere near the store.

"Let's show Mommy now, Daddy!" Grace chirped and danced a jig. Duke barked.

Molly's heart melted at the sound of Grace calling her Mommy. She had a feeling she'd have that reaction to it for the rest of her life. "Yeah, come on, Daddy!" Molly laughed and tried to tug on her blindfold.

"Okay, let me get this off. But keep your eyes shut until I tell you to open them." His fingers fiddled with the scarf tied securely around her head.

"Hurry!" The anticipation was killing her.

"I'm trying, but there's a big knot. I can't get it—"

Cheerful lighting blinded her when the scarf dropped to the ground. "Oh my! It's beautiful!"

Molly threw her hands over her mouth. The place was enormous. The wall once dividing her store with Derek's coffee shop was gone, leaving behind a large open floor plan.

"It's all one place, Mommy." Grace swung her arms wide open, dropped the leash and twirled. "You and Daddy get to work together now. I can help, too, when I'm not in school."

Molly moved through the shop to make sure it wasn't a dream. The selection of books was larger, and the children's section had doubled in size. She gasped and pointed to the brightly colored rocking chairs. "Look how many there are!"

Derek stepped beside his wife. "I know how important Book Buddies is to you. Plus, I figured if we make room for more kids, it would mean more parents in the store shopping."

Taking in her surroundings, Molly was filled with joy. She turned to Derek. "You are brilliant, you know? This is such a natural pairing, books and coffee. They go together." She pointed at the large sign over the counter. "And the name—Caffeinated Reads—it's genius."

"Well, I figured since we got married, why not marry our businesses?" Derek slid his arm around her waist, and she melted against his muscular frame. "So you like it?"

"Like? I love it. It's the perfect wedding gift.

I think it might be a good time to share the surprise we have for Daddy. Don't you think, Grace?" Molly flashed a smile and peered over at Grace.

"Let me guess. I'm not going to be forced to eat mushrooms on my pizza anymore?" Derek winked.

Molly laughed and shook her head. "Do you want to tell him, Grace?"

The child bounced up and down. Her face beamed. "Yes! Yes! I'm going to have a baby brother or a baby sister, Daddy."

Molly watched as Derek's mouth fell open and his eyes widened.

"We're going to be the family I've always prayed for," Grace exclaimed, and a tear of joy rolled down her cheek.

* * * * *

If you enjoyed this story, don't miss Jill Weatherholt's next sweet romance, available next year from Love Inspired!

Find more great reads at www.LoveInspired.com

Dear Reader,

Writing a book is always a challenge. When I first began to write Molly and Derek's story, I was going to my day job each day and visiting with family and friends. Life was routine, at times mundane. But it was the life I knew and it was good. When COVID-19 took the world by surprise, my world changed in ways I'd never imagined. I'm sure yours did, too.

As weeks turned into months, one thing didn't change—my trust in God. Like Molly, who believed it was part of God's plan for her to bring Grace into her home, I knew I could rest my worried mind in the truth that God always has a plan for us. It might not always make sense, but in the end, it will all work out for our good.

I hope you enjoyed revisiting Whispering Slopes as much as I did. In times such as these, being able to write happy endings to share with all of you is truly a gift from God.

I love to connect with readers. Please sign up for my newsletter at JillWeatherholt.com. I'd love to chat.

Jill Weatherholt

Get 4 FREE REWARDS!

We'll send you 2 FREE Books plus 2 FREE Mystery Gifts.

Love Inspired Suspense books showcase how courage and optimism unite in stories of faith and love in the face of danger.

FREE Value Over **$20**

Get 4 **FREE REWARDS!**

We'll send you 2 FREE Books <u>plus</u> 2 FREE Mystery Gifts.

Harlequin Heartwarming Larger-Print books will connect you to uplifting stories where the bonds of friendship, family and community unite.

FREE Value Over **$20**

YES! Please send me 2 FREE Harlequin Heartwarming Larger-Print novels and my 2 FREE mystery gifts (gifts worth about $10 retail). After receiving them, if I don't wish to receive any more books, I can return the shipping statement marked "cancel." If I don't cancel, I will receive 4 brand-new larger-print novels every month and be billed just $5.74 per book in the U.S. or $6.24 per book in Canada. That's a savings of at least 21% off the cover price. It's quite a bargain! Shipping and handling is just 50¢ per book in the U.S. and $1.25 per book in Canada.* I understand that accepting the 2 free books and gifts places me under no obligation to buy anything. I can always return a shipment and cancel at any time. The free books and gifts are mine to keep no matter what I decide.

161/361 HDN GNPZ

Name (please print)

Address   Apt. #

City   State/Province   Zip/Postal Code

Email: Please check this box ☐ if you would like to receive newsletters and promotional emails from Harlequin Enterprises ULC and its affiliates. You can unsubscribe anytime.

Mail to the **Harlequin Reader Service:**
IN U.S.A.: P.O. Box 1341, Buffalo, NY 14240-8531
IN CANADA: P.O. Box 603, Fort Erie, Ontario L2A 5X3

Want to try 2 free books from another series? Call 1-800-873-8635 or visit www.ReaderService.com.

---

*Terms and prices subject to change without notice. Prices do not include sales taxes, which will be charged (if applicable) based on your state or country of residence. Canadian residents will be charged applicable taxes. Offer not valid in Quebec. This offer is limited to one order per household. Books received may not be as shown. Not valid for current subscribers to Harlequin Heartwarming Larger-Print books. All orders subject to approval. Credit or debit balances in a customer's account(s) may be offset by any other outstanding balance owed by or to the customer. Please allow 4 to 6 weeks for delivery. Offer available while quantities last.

Your Privacy—Your information is being collected by Harlequin Enterprises ULC, operating as Harlequin Reader Service. For a complete summary of the information we collect, how we use this information and to whom it is disclosed, please visit our privacy notice located at corporate.harlequin.com/privacy-notice. From time to time we may also exchange your personal information with reputable third parties. If you wish to opt out of this sharing of your personal information, please visit readerservice.com/consumerschoice or call 1-800-873-8635. **Notice to California Residents**—Under California law, you have specific rights to control and access your data. For more information on these rights and how to exercise them, visit corporate.harlequin.com/california-privacy.

HW21R

COMING NEXT MONTH FROM
Love Inspired

COURTING HIS AMISH WIFE
by Emma Miller
When Levi Miller learns Eve Summy is about to be forced to marry her would-be attacker or risk being shunned, he marries her instead. Now husband and wife, but complete strangers, the two have to figure out how to live together in harmony...and maybe even find love along the way.

HER PATH TO REDEMPTION
by Patrice Lewis
Returning to the Amish community she left during her *rumspringa*, widowed mother Eliza Struder's determined to redeem the wild reputation of her youth. But one woman stands between her and acceptance into the church—the mother of the man she left behind. Can she convince the community—and Josiah Lapp—to give her a second chance?

THE COWGIRL'S SACRIFICE
Hearts of Oklahoma • by Tina Radcliffe
Needing time to heal after a rodeo injury, Kate Rainbolt heads to her family ranch to accept the foreman job her brothers offered her months ago. But the position's already been filled by her ex-boyfriend, Jess McNally. With Jess as her boss—and turning into something more—this wandering cowgirl might finally put down roots...

A FUTURE TO FIGHT FOR
Bliss, Texas • by Mindy Obenhaus
Single father Crockett Devereaux and widow Paisley Wainwright can't get through a church-committee meeting without arguing—and now they have to work together to turn a local castle into a museum and wedding venue. But first they must put their differences aside...and realize they make the perfect team.

THE MISSIONARY'S PURPOSE
Small Town Sisterhood • by Kat Brookes
Wounded and back home after a mission trip, Jake Landers never expected his estranged friend Addy Mitchell to offer help. She hurt him by keeping secrets, and he's not sure he can trust her. But when their friendship sparks into love, can he forgive her...and give her his heart?

FINDING HER COURAGE
by Christine Raymond
Inheriting part of a ranch is an answer to prayers for struggling widow Camille Bellamy and her little girl—except Ty Spencer was left the rest of it. They strike a bargain: he'll agree to sell the ranch if she helps plan an event that could keep his business afloat. But can their arrangement stay strictly professional?

———

LOOK FOR THESE AND OTHER LOVE INSPIRED BOOKS WHEREVER BOOKS ARE SOLD, INCLUDING MOST BOOKSTORES, SUPERMARKETS, DISCOUNT STORES AND DRUGSTORES.

LICNM0721